WHAT A WEEK TO MAKE A STAND

ROSIE RUSHTON

PUFFIN BOOKS

PUFFIN BOOKS

Published by the Penguin Group
Penguin Books Ltd, 80 Strand, London WC2R 0RL, England
Penguin Putnam Inc., 375 Hudson Street, New York, New York 10014, USA
Penguin Books Australia Ltd, 250 Camberwell Road, Camberwell, Victoria 3124,
Australia
Penguin Books Canada Ltd, 10 Alcorn Avenue, Toronto, Ontario, Canada M4V 3B2
Penguin Books India (P) Ltd, 11 Community Centre, Panchsheel Park,
New Delhi – 110 017, India
Penguin Books (NZ) Ltd, Cnr Rosedale and Airborne Roads, Albany, Auckland,
New Zealand
Penguin Books (South Africa) (Pty) Ltd, 24 Sturdee Avenue, Rosebank 2196,
South Africa

Penguin Books Ltd, Registered Offices: 80 Strand, London WC2R 0RL, England

www.penguin.com

First published 1999
4

Text copyright © Rosie Rushton, 1999
All rights reserved

The moral right of the author has been asserted

Set in 10pt /14pt Folio

Made and printed in England by Clays Ltd, St Ives plc

British Library Cataloguing in Publication Data
A CIP catalogue record for this book is available from the British Library

ISBN 0-141-30225-9

Acclaim for Rosie Rushton's books

...ting comedy' – *The Times*

...ut sure-footed, the humour,
...avy-breathing is juggled with
...ce of wit and sympathy'
– *Guardian*

...nable' – *Bliss* magazine

...ad ... belly-achingly funny'
19 magazine

Some other books by Rosie Rushton

(in reading order by series)
WHAT A WEEK TO FALL IN LOVE
WHAT A WEEK TO MAKE IT BIG
WHAT A WEEK TO BREAK FREE
WHAT A WEEK TO PLAY IT COOL
WHAT A WEEK TO MAKE A MOVE

For older readers

OLIVIA
SOPHIE
MELISSA
POPPY
JESSICA

JUST DON'T MAKE A SCENE, MUM!
I THINK I'LL JUST CURL UP AND DIE
HOW COULD YOU DO THIS TO ME, MUM?
DOES ANYONE ROUND HERE EVER LISTEN?

MONDAY

7.00 a.m.

In the kitchen of 6 Kestrel Close, West Green, Dunchester. Thankful it's Monday

Cleo Greenway stood at the kitchen window, staring out at the driving rain and trying very hard to think of something nice.

She had read this feature in *Heaven* magazine that said when you felt stressed out, you should close your eyes and imagine yourself lying on a beach under a waving palm tree. She supposed it must work for some people, otherwise they wouldn't be allowed to print it, but it wasn't doing anything for her. This might have something to do, she supposed, with the fact that being chubby, she didn't like to dwell on situations which involved swimsuits and bare flesh. She guessed her friends would get relaxation techniques to work first go. Not that they would need to. For one thing, they didn't get into a state all the time like she did and, for another, they didn't live in the war zone that was 6 Kestrel Close.

As if to prove her point, the early morning silence was

1

shattered by the slamming of a door and the sound of her sixteen-year-old sister's strident tones echoing across the landing.

'Mum! Lettie's messed with my make-up again!'

'Oh, Lettie, precious ...' Mrs Greenway's well-modulated voice floated from her bedroom.

'I didn't, it wasn't me!' Lettie, aged eleven going on four and a half, was doing her hard-done-by infant routine. 'It was Cleo – I saw her.'

'I'll kill her!' stormed Portia, to the sound of slamming drawers. 'She's knackered my new lip liner! Cleeeee-oh!'

'Will you two pack it in?' The gravelly tones of Roy, their stepfather, resounded across the landing. 'Why does everyone in this house have to make a drama out of a crisis?'

'But Cleo's taken my –'

'Then sort Cleo out – but for pity's sake, do it quietly!' The bedroom door slammed, followed in quick succession by the bathroom door and a manic clanking of pipes as the shower was turned on full blast.

Oh charming, thought Cleo, checking out the fridge for something resembling breakfast. As if she would bother to borrow Portia's precious lip liner! Her sister might not mind looking as if she had the contents of a jar of Marmite on her lips but Cleo favoured the understated look. The more understated the better. That way, people were less likely to notice you were there. As for Lettie, the little toad, how dare she tell lies about her! There were times when Cleo wished fervently that she was an only child.

Not, of course, she thought guiltily, that she didn't love her family. It was just that they were so ... well, there. But then again, she wouldn't have wanted to be in Jade's position. Jade Williams didn't have a family at all – not one of her own. Her parents had been killed in a road accident a few months before, and Jade now lived with her aunt, Paula, and her family. She'd had a pretty tough time settling down – but despite all that, Jade was gutsy and spunky, and had even been known to do things like cutting off all her hair and dying it burnished copper. When Jade didn't like something, she did her best to change it; she was so together. In fact, Cleo mused sadly, all her friends were more together than she was.

It would be so cool, she thought, abandoning her fridge search and grabbing a packet of cereal from the cupboard, to be like Holly Vine. Holly was tall and willowy and never worried about anything, except perhaps where her next boyfriend was coming from. Her parents were pretty ancient, but they never seemed to argue or slam doors. Holly said that was because her father was too busy writing about the Civil War and living in the past to notice anything that was happening in the present – and her mum was so bossy that she just did her own thing regardless. Cleo's mum had a tendency to do her own thing too – only lately Roy, her stepfather, didn't seem to like it very much. And when Roy wasn't happy, *everyone* knew about it.

Life might be easier, thought Cleo, shaking cereal into a bowl, if she was more like Tansy Meadows, who was tiny, athletic and very clever and knew exactly where she was going in life and how she was going to get there. Tansy didn't have a dad, step or otherwise – or, at least, not one that she had ever seen – and she lived with her mum, Clarity, in a cute little cottage with wonky floorboards and no irritating sisters to wind her up. Tansy's mum was into

New Age thinking, which meant she didn't agree with raised voices or disturbed auras.

In this house, thought Cleo, prising open a milk carton, an aura wouldn't have time to appear, never mind get disturbed. Tansy had assured Cleo that having a laid-back mother did have its disadvantages, like the electricity getting cut off because she had forgotten to pay the bill, and the small matter of not quite knowing who Tansy's father was. She said that Clarity said no just as often as every other short-sighted parent, but just did it quietly. My family, thought Cleo, slumping down at the kitchen table, never do anything quietly.

She fiddled with a stray strand of honey-blonde hair and wished for the hundredth time that she was more like her friends. None of them would have been wandering around the house since five-thirty when they could have been tucked up in bed. But then none of them kept having The Dream.

Cleo shivered, not because it was cold, but because she could not shake off the awful feelings that always followed her dream. She had had it off and on for almost as long as she could remember; when she was little, she used to scream out in the night, and her mum would rush in and cuddle her and ask her why she was crying, but she could never put it into words because all the images got muddled. As she got older, her family got used to the odd cry in the night and took little notice – although once Lettie had padded along from her bedroom, put her skinny arms round her and asked her what was wrong. But, of course, she couldn't tell her. She couldn't tell anyone. But least of all Lettie.

Cleo knew that her mum loved Lettie the most. She

guessed that was because of what had happened to her and because she was the baby of the family. Baby was about right, Cleo thought – and immediately felt guilty again. After all, it wasn't Lettie's fault that she was in a class a year below her age, or that she got made a fuss of because she walked with a limp. She shouldn't think horrible things about her younger sister – she should be extra nice to her to make up for ...

Stop it, she admonished herself, draining the last dregs of milk from her bowl. Stop thinking about it. If you don't think about it, maybe the dream won't come back. Think of something nice.

Like the fact that it was Monday. She knew her friends would be amazed to discover that just thinking about the whole five days of school ahead of her before the weekend came round again made Cleo feel better. Holly, Tansy and Jade all lived for weekends: Cleo lived for them to be over.

And this one had been worse than most. It wasn't just that her mum and Roy had spent half of Saturday arguing about money; that had been happening a lot lately. Cleo adored her mum, but even she had to admit that she had no head for figures. Whenever she got bored, or something went just the slightest bit wrong, Diana Greenway sped off to the nearest clothes shop, waving her credit card and seeking solace among the rails of silk shirts and designer dresses. And then, when the bill finally arrived, she would gaze at it in genuine horror and cry, 'How on earth did that happen?'

'It happened,' Roy had said through clenched teeth over breakfast on Saturday morning, when Diana had again expressed astonishment at Barclaycard's arithmetical calculations, 'because of your total inability to live within your means. It might help if you got a proper job, instead of indulging in all these exhibitionist shenanigans.'

Cleo's mum had looked wounded.

'But, Roy darling, this Fittinix TV advert is a godsend – it could be the start of a whole new career!' she had protested, nibbling daintily on a calorie-reduced crispbread as befitted the woman who had been selected to model figure-enhancing knickers in front of the entire viewing population of the United Kingdom.

'Oh yes?' Roy had retorted sarcastically, irritation clouding his rugged features. 'Like that walk-on part in Coronation Street was going to make you a TV star?'

He had caught sight of his wife's downcast expression and softened.

'Look, Di love, I know how keen you are on this acting lark, but you've got to get real. We're in a mess financially. You don't want us to have to sell the house, do you?'

Cleo had gasped. She knew Roy went on and on about money not growing on trees, and moaned that Max, Cleo's real dad, didn't send enough money each month to cover what he called the 'girls' ridiculous outgoings', but she hadn't thought it was that serious.

To her relief, her mother had burst out laughing.

'Oh, Roy darling, really!' she had exclaimed, shoving the credit card bill under the toast rack. 'Sell the house, indeed! As if! You are too, too dramatic. This is just a teeny blip and as soon –'

To Cleo's horror, Roy had pushed back his chair, stood up and thumped his fist on the table. Even Portia, who made ignoring other people into an art form, had been sufficiently moved to elevate a razor-thin eyebrow heavenwards.

'When are you going to start living in the real world? This isn't a play with a happy ending, this is life!' he had shouted. 'I am fed up with working my fingers to the bone to support you and your kids, while you go for months on end without contributing a penny. I don't know how much more I can take!'

Cleo's chest had tightened. She had heard similar words before – often. Her father used to say the same thing years earlier, before he left to go and live with Fleur on a barge on the Norfolk Broads. She had never been quite sure what it was he couldn't take, but she remembered quite well that her mum had been devastated, crying and not eating; Portia had played truant from school and Lettie had regressed to the age of about four, from which era she had still to emerge. If Roy left as well, Cleo dreaded to think what they would do.

Which was why she had spent the rest of the weekend trying to telephone her father. If she could just explain to him about the money situation, she was sure he would send more cash. But every time she had rung his mobile, it had been switched to answerphone. It was still like that this morning. What made it worse was that her father had promised to ring on Sunday and now she was worried that he was ill or had fallen off the boat or crashed his car.

She didn't want to say anything to her mum, because she knew it would make her flip and start one of her 'I always said that man had no sense of responsibility' outbursts. There was no point in telling Portia, because Portia told everyone she hated her father. She had never forgiven him for taking up with Fleur, who was only twenty-eight and almost young enough to be their sister. Portia said Fleur was a man-snatcher and a bimbo and Lettie said she smelt, which, like most of what came out of Lettie's mouth, was ridiculous. Secretly, Cleo rather liked Fleur. Not that it would be wise to admit it, of course. Whenever she went to visit her dad, Fleur never hung around trying to be all matey-matey; she never suggested outings to theme parks where you had to ride on scary log flumes; and she never asked searching questions about your love life. Which, thought Cleo now, deliberating about whether to have a second bowl of cereal or a buttered croissant, was just as well, because she was pretty sure that hers was about to take a nosedive.

Until last week, thinking about Trig Roscoe would definitely have qualified under the heading of Something Nice. Now it fitted better under Something Very Worrying. She loved him so much – really passionately, toe-jerkingly adored him. They had been going out long enough for everyone to see them as an item; he had told her she was lovely, which she knew wasn't true, but was nice to hear all the same, and at the disco during their school field trip he had admitted how he really felt about her. But just recently he hadn't been phoning her every evening, and instead of ambling home from school with her, he had dashed off without a word. What if he had got someone else? What if he wanted someone more trendy, more fun to be with? If she lost him, she would die.

Which was why she had decided at precisely five forty-five this morning that she was going to change. Dramatically. She was fed up with being boring old Cleo, the one who always hung back on the sidelines, scared that something awful was about to happen, sad old Cleo who always came up with reasons why not to do things. From now on, she thought, taking the croissant out of the microwave and sinking her teeth into the oozing butter, she was going to be like her friends and live for the moment. She was going to stop worrying and go with the flow. And this was definitely the week to do it.

After all, she and Trig would be seeing even more of one another than usual. West Green Upper School's choir, of which they were both members, had made it to the finals of *In Voice*, the Midlands Schools Festival of Song, which meant rehearsals after school and, hopefully, a return to those slow, smoochy walks home.

Fired with determination, she stood up, closed her eyes, puckered her lips and wrapped her arms around her chest by way of kissing practice. She had just got to the interesting, murmuring bit when the kitchen door swung open, hitting her in the chest and causing her to spit croissant crumbs all down her sweater.

'Sweetheart, darling lamb, you're up and dressed already!' Cleo's mother swept in on a cloud of Allure. She was wearing skin-tight cappuccino-coloured leather trousers and a lycra body and looked considerably younger than her forty-five years. 'Isn't it too too depressing about this ghastly weather? Honestly, the elements are so unkind!'

Diana Greenway could never quite forget the fact that for two seasons back in the late Seventies she had been one of the lesser lights of the Royal Shakespeare Company, and not content with naming her daughters after Shakespearean heroines, she managed to make the most mundane event take on the proportions of one the Bard's epic tragedies.

'I quite like rain,' commented Cleo, wiping crumbs off her school uniform. 'Rain means games get cancelled.'

Cleo was of the firm belief that any activity involving running, jumping or otherwise exposing large areas of undisciplined flesh was quite uncalled for.

'Never mind games, angel face,' said her mother, pouring boiling water on to a herbal tea bag. 'We are due to film the Fittinix ad this week.'

'So?' said Cleo. 'What has the weather got to do with that? You'll be in a studio.'

'Darling, no, didn't I tell you?' Diana sat down at the table and rested her chin in her immaculately manicured hands. 'It's all so thrilling – the agency came up with a brilliant idea. I'm going to hang out of a balloon.'

Cleo paused in mid-bite, her own troubles fading in the face of the enormity of her mother's most recent revelation.

'You are going to *what*?'

'I'm going ballooning, sweetheart,' affirmed her mother. 'It's so clever – there are going to be shots of the balloon drifting over the ruins of Dunchester Castle, and close-ups of women in period costume being laced into their corsets – all gasping and panting, darling, and going "ouch", you know what I mean? – and then suddenly the camera will zoom into the balloon and there I'll be in the Fittinix gear, and a voice will say "Put Pain in the Past and Firm up with Fittinix – the gasp-free control pant." Don't you think that's splendid?'

Cleo stared at her mother in disbelief.

'You mean, do I think it's splendid that my mother is going to be floating over Dunchester hanging out of a balloon in her underwear? In full view of everyone?'

Diana nodded enthusiastically. 'I knew you'd be thrilled,' she said.

'Oh, positively delirious,' muttered Cleo. 'And when is this mind-blowing event due to take place?'

'As soon as we get the right weather, darling,' said her mother. 'I know, you could bring some of your friends along to watch!'

I don't believe she just said that, thought Cleo. This is it – my mother has finally gone over the edge. She has totally lost the power of rational thought.

'No thanks,' she replied hastily. 'I'll be busy.'

'Busy, darling? You?' Diana made it sound about as unlikely as Cleo winning the Nobel Prize for Literature. 'How come?'

'Mum, I've told you a hundred times already – it's the choir finals.'

'Oh, of course. Rehearsals at all hours, I suppose. Is that why you're ready so early?'

Cleo bit her lip and wondered whether she dared try to talk to her mum.

'Not really,' she said. 'The thing is, I've been awake since five.'

'Darling!' Diana looked horrified. 'How awful for you! Lack of sleep does terrible things to the complexion. I'm a martyr to puffy eyes myself. Tell you what, you can borrow my Replenishing Gel with Aloe Vera – it's wonderful stuff and –'

Cleo tried again. 'No, Mum, listen – I had that dream again,' she said in a rush. 'The one where I'm in the car and then ...'

Her voice faltered.

Her mother put her hand to her mouth, glanced at her swiftly and then went to the door.

'Portia! Lettie! Come along now, it's getting late!'

She's doing it again, thought Cleo with a sinking heart. She's deliberately changing the subject. Why wouldn't her

11

mum let her talk about it? If only she could remember ...

'Darling, everyone has bad dreams from time to time,' her mother interjected briskly, flinging slices of granary bread into the toaster. 'Just put it out of your mind – that's what I do.'

'But it won't go out of my mind,' protested Cleo. 'It's horrid, it's –'

'Oh, Lettie lambkin, there you are! And Portia – what have you done to your hair?'

Diana turned towards the door, obviously judging the maroon streak that had appeared in her eldest daughter's hair to be a safer topic for early morning discussion than Cleo's nocturnal imaginings.

Suddenly Cleo didn't want to be there; she didn't want to look at Portia in her size-eight clothes and be reminded yet again that she was the only one who hadn't inherited their mother's sylphlike figure. She didn't want to sit next to Lettie, because every time she looked at her, bits of the dream came back and they weren't nice bits.

'Cleo, darling, just do Lettie's braid for me, will you?' chirruped her mother, furiously buttering toast. 'Oh, and have you fed Peaseblossom? You know how cross it makes Roy if the cat gets under his feet at breakfast time.'

'No, no and what a pity!' Cleo almost gasped audibly at her own audacity.

'Cleo?' Diana looked as astonished as Cleo felt.

'Sorry, but I haven't got time to do hair and feed cats – I've got to dash,' she said as cheerfully as she could. 'Catch you later.'

'But, Cleo, it's only half-past seven – and besides, I just wanted you to –'

But Cleo didn't wait to hear what anyone just wanted.

She sped along the hall, grabbed her raincoat off the hook and picked up her school bag. As she opened the front door she heard her mother's voice raised in protest.

'I can't think what's got into her,' she said. 'That's not like our Cleo, not a bit.'

Cleo stopped trying to think about something nice. Nothing could be nicer than hearing her mother say just that. The old Cleo was on the way out.

7.30 a.m.

**In her bedroom at The Cedars, Weston Way, West Green.
Brooding on thwarted plans**

As Cleo's determination soared, so Holly Vine's spirits began spiralling downwards at an alarming rate.

It was typical of her life to date, she thought, leaning her elbows on her bedroom windowsill and staring angrily out at the rain, that on the one occasion that she had managed to come up with a scheme for sorting out the mess that was her love life, the weather had to go and ruin it all.

She really had thought she had it sussed this time; she had planned to leave early for school and then sit on the bit of broken wall at the end of Weston Way, legs crossed attractively, her freshly shampooed nutmeg-brown hair flowing over her left shoulder, waiting for Paul. He would saunter past on his way to catch the bus, stop, turn, gaze open-mouthed at her stunning beauty and wonder immediately how he could have been so crazy as to ignore her very existence for the last five days. He would open his arms, she would jump daintily off the wall, and they would be folded in one long, lingering kiss. And all thoughts of The Girl would leave his mind for ever.

Holly was exceedingly worried about The Girl. She didn't know her name, but what little she did know about her was troubling enough. For one thing, she went to Bishop Agnew College, which gave her a head start over Holly straight away. It was all right for Cleo, Tansy and Jade – the guys they fancied all went to West Green Upper, where they could see them every day and fend off any competition before it was too late. Paul Bennett was at the town's posh private school, which meant he and Holly caught different buses and came home at different times. When Paul had asked her out, she had assumed they would see heaps of one another, what with his family living in the new house that had been built in what had once been Holly's vegetable garden. But it wasn't working out like that. In fact, she couldn't even peer into his house from her bedroom and have a quick drool because his mum had encased the whole place in upmarket vertical blinds and swathes of muslin drapes. So ever since their first date, Holly, ever resourceful, had got into the habit of just happening to be hanging around when the Bishop Agnew bus pulled up in the evenings – which was when she had seen Paul and The Girl together. Rather too together for Holly's liking.

She had taken one look at the way Paul was leaning towards the girl, hanging on her every word, and hated her on sight. She was short enough to be able to tilt her chin and gaze upwards into Paul's eyes; Holly was exactly the same height as Paul and had to sag at the knees when she wanted to look in need of manly protection. This girl might be tiny but she had the sort of chest that seemed to be engaged in a constant struggle to escape from her tight-fitting sweater; Holly's boobs were lopsided, which meant she had to wear baggy jumpers in the hope that no one would guess.

When Paul had leaned towards the girl and tilted her chin with his finger, she had decided enough was enough.

'Hi, Paul!' she had called, trying to make her voice sound husky and alluring. 'Coming round later?'

Paul had turned, smiled briefly and shaken his head, flicking a shock of fair hair from his eyes. He hadn't even had the good grace to look guilty.

'Sorry,' he had called back. 'Can't make it tonight.'

Holly knew that at this point she should have taken notice of all the advice in her magazines, tossed her head, looked unconcerned and strolled serenely away. But Holly wasn't into being serene.

'How come?' she had demanded, catching up with the pair and determinedly ignoring the girl's puzzled looks. 'I hardly ever see you.'

Paul had sighed impatiently.

'I've just got things to do – it's no big deal,' he said.

Holly had wanted to say that anything which took precedence over an evening with her was a very big deal indeed, but she had been acutely aware of the girl staring at her intently with huge aquamarine eyes. She was sickeningly pretty in a porcelain doll kind of way, with long, thick flaxen-coloured hair and a pale skin which looked terrific against the expensive-looking charcoal-grey hooded trench coat she was wearing. Obviously she was the posey type, thought Holly bitterly; covering up Bishop Agnew's purple and cream uniform with something that definitely had a designer label. Holly had given her what she hoped was a long, mean stare and had been about to sidle closer to Paul when he turned back to the girl.

'Come on,' he had said, jerking his head in the direction of his house. 'I don't know about you but I'm starved.'

Holly had watched in misery as the two of them had turned into the driveway of Paul's house. Then she had run full pelt down her own path, through the front door and up to her bedroom. Flinging open the window, she had gazed in ever-increasing agony at the house which had just been built in what had once been their vegetable garden. Paul's house. It should be her in there with him, not someone else. She had stood there for ages, imagining what might be going on behind those leaded-light windows and drawn curtains. Were they laughing at her behind her back? Was he kissing her? Worse still, was she about to get dumped?

She had been thinking similar thoughts ever since. What made it worse was that the weekend before she had been thwarted in her attempts to see him, because on Friday night the whole family had leaped into the car and disappeared, towing a trailer tent behind them.

'Well, at least he won't be seeing this girl then,' Tansy had reasoned when Holly had phoned her to ask whether you really could die of a broken heart. 'And by the time he gets back, he'll probably be missing you like crazy.'

'Missing her more like,' Holly had moaned. 'He hasn't even phoned me.'

'Boys are like that,' Tansy had replied knowledgeably. 'They're not hot on communication skills.'

'Well, he didn't seem to be making a bad job of communicating with her,' Holly had retorted. 'Maybe I'll put a note through his door for when he gets back and –'

'No way!' Tansy had exploded at the other end of the

phone. 'What you have to do is play it icy cool. Show him you don't care what he does.'

'But I do!' Holly had protested tearfully.

'I know, but the last person to tell is Paul,' persisted Tansy. 'What you need is a strategy.'

Which was how, despite constant interruptions from Holly's mother who apparently could not see the need for her daughter to tie up the phone lines for half an hour when there was biology course work to be attended to, they had come up with the sitting on the wall idea.

'But it won't work unless you look aloof,' Tansy had told her firmly. 'And if he asks you what sort of a weekend you had, you have to close your eyes, give yourself a hug and say "Wonderful" in a breathy kind of voice.'

'Why?' asked Holly.

'Because, silly, he'll immediately feel jealous and wonder what on earth you've been up to without him. That will mean –'

Quite what it would mean, Holly didn't find out because her mother, whose limited patience had finally expired, had yanked the receiver from her hand and gone on at great length about it being a pity that Holly didn't expend as much energy over her homework as she did thinking about boys. Which was grossly unfair. What her mother seemed incapable of understanding was that Holly couldn't possibly concentrate on the life cycle of the lesser-spotted toad while some stuck-up kid was trying to get her hands on her boyfriend. That was the downside of having an old mother; their minds starting going before you had grown up.

It would be so nice, thought Holly now, deftly applying Charismatic Coral lip liner, to have a mother who got her priorities right. If Angela Vine wasn't always so busy writing to newspapers, counselling fallen women and organizing protest marches, she might have actually got round to inviting Paul's mum over for coffee. And then Paul's mum would invite her back and in next to no time, both families would be in and out of one another's houses, and Holly and Paul would see one another every day and ...

That was it! It was all down to her mother. She would have to be made to see that it was her social and moral duty to be friendly to the new neighbours. Never mind painting the crèche at the Lowdown Centre or taking busloads of kids to Clacton, it was time Angela Vine did a few good works closer to home. And what was more, if she could get her to see sense right away, Holly could go across with the invitation before Paul left for school. There was no time to waste.

She hurtled downstairs, scooping her nutmeg-brown hair back into a black scrunchie, and pushed open the kitchen door, almost falling over Naseby, her father's Lilac Burmese cat who was sulking because Rupert Vine was away lecturing in America and no one else in the house was prepared to feed him salmon and double cream for breakfast. Holly's mother, who would have been doing maternal things like boiling eggs or buttering toast if she had been a halfway normal parent, was kneeling in the middle of the kitchen floor, surrounded by pieces of white cardboard and a somewhat battered *Captain Pugwash* annual. Of breakfast there was no sign.

'Oh, Holly dear, there you are, thank goodness. Put the coffee on, will you? I'm parched.'

Angela Vine struggled to her feet, ran her fingers distractedly through her greying hair and eyed the litter-strewn floor.

'It's no good, something's missing,' she said as Holly scooped coffee into the cafetiere. 'Darling, pull up your shirt a minute, will you?'

Holly stared at her mother.

'Do *what*?'

'I want to count your ribs, dear. For my skeleton.'

Holly banged the cafetiere on to the hob and slumped into the nearest chair.

'Mum, would you mind telling me what you are on about? What's with all this junk on the floor?'

'That's it, dear. I'm making a skeleton. Only I can't seem to get it right. Now just lift up your top, Holly, there's a dear.'

She reached out a hand to her daughter's sweater.

'Get off!' snapped Holly. 'Count your own ribs.'

'I wish,' sighed her mother. 'Too much middle-age spread to find the damn things, I'm afraid. I don't mean to be intrusive, darling – but I've got to get this finished for the sit-in.'

Holly cringed.

'Oh no – don't tell me you are going to make a public spectacle of yourself yet again,' she pleaded. 'Haven't you done enough for one lifetime?'

The awful memory of her mother being arrested by the local constabulary while dressed as a white rabbit was still too close for comfort.

'Holly, it's that attitude that has got this country into the mess we face today,' said her mother fiercely, pouring coffee into a mug. 'Did you know that Dunchester Hospital's casualty department might have to close? Now where would your father's foot have been without Casualty?'

'On the end of his leg as usual, I imagine,' muttered Holly, peering into a packet of wheat flakes and finding it empty. Her father's encounter with the wrong end of a pikestaff while careering about in an unseemly manner with the Sealed Knot Society a few weeks before was another memory Holly preferred to erase from her mind.

'Don't be flippant, Holly,' admonished her mother. 'He's still in a lot of pain. Anyway, these cutbacks are an outrage. It's at times like this I wish I had gone into politics instead of –'

'Instead of having me, you mean?' snapped Holly, taking a slice of bread from the bread bin and examining it for mould. 'I am so sorry I got born just when you were going to get elected. So sorry I was an afterthought, wrecking your plans ...'

Her mother gave her a hug.

'That's not what I meant, and you know it,' she said. 'I wouldn't be without you for the world. It's just that the government needs people like me.'

Angela Vine had many attributes; undue modesty was not one of them.

'This bread's stale,' said Holly, wishing that her mother's housekeeping skills were on a par with her political know-how.

'Have some crispbread,' said her mother.

'Oh great,' said Holly.

'Anyway,' continued Mrs Vine briskly, ignoring her daughter's need for sustenance, 'we're organizing a sit-in and I thought we could carry a huge skeleton and hang it in the entrance. With a slogan, darling, you know, something like "put the flesh back on our health service." I say – that's rather good, don't you think?'

Holly thought this didn't warrant a reply.

'Listen, Mum, before you get into all that, I really think you ought to go and see Paul's mum. I mean, this business about hospitals and sit-ins is all very well, but you are their neighbour, after all, and you ought to –'

'Holly!' Her mother turned and enveloped her in a huge bear hug. 'Darling, you're a star! Why didn't I think of that? Of course! Deannie Bennett! Oh hallelujah!'

I was too late, thought Holly, as her mother danced across the kitchen floor and yanked open the fridge door. My mother is certifiably insane.

'This could be the answer to all my prayers,' declared Angela, cracking eggs into the frying pan at great speed. 'She'd be able to do one in five minutes, wouldn't she?'

A nasty niggle edged its way into Holly's mind.

'Do what?'

'Make a skeleton, sweetheart,' said her mum, throwing some bacon on top of the eggs. 'You were so clever. Who better to ask than an art teacher?'

'That's not what I ...' Holly opened her mouth to protest, thought for a minute, and then closed it again. She had forgotten that Paul's mum taught art at evening classes; and the thought of her mother hurtling over there and talking gibberish about protests and skeletons was hardly what she had in mind. It wouldn't help her cause if Mrs Bennett realized that her son was going out with the daughter of a nutcase. On the other hand, it was a start; and at least Holly would have an excuse to call in later, if only to apologize for her mother's behaviour. And it did appear that breakfast might after all materialize.

'You will behave, won't you?' Holly said firmly. 'I mean, you won't get on your high horse and go on about politics and stuff? And you're not to talk about me, you understand? And promise me you won't do anything embarrassing.'

'Oh, Holly,' sighed her mum, flipping an egg over in the pan. 'As if I would. I shall just be my normal natural self.'

'That,' said Holly with a deep sigh, 'is what worries me.'

7.45 a.m.

In the kitchen of 3 Plough Cottages, Cattle Hill, West Green, Dunchester

It would be rather nice, thought Tansy Meadows, removing a packet of what appeared to be decomposing seaweed from the fridge and grabbing the last yoghurt, to have a parent who wasn't a constant and ongoing source of worry. Of course, the chances would have been doubled had she had the full quota of parents, but since her father had seen fit to disappear into the dark blue yonder soon after her conception, she had no way of knowing just how he stood on the sanity front. But, she thought, ripping the top off her yoghurt, she must have got her own brains from someone, and judging on present performance it certainly wasn't her mother.

'There you are, my little one,' Clarity cooed. 'You just nestle down in there and then in no time at all, we'll have you all snugly in a nice warm bed.'

Tansy raised her eyes heavenwards and sighed deeply.

'Mum,' she said with exaggerated patience, 'it is bad enough having to stand up to eat my breakfast because you have the entire contents of a greenhouse spread over the

22

kitchen table, but do you have to hold conversations with seedlings? People have been locked up for less.'

Her mother ran a compost-encrusted hand through her auburn frizz and eyed Tansy earnestly.

'No, darling, it's a proven fact – plants like to be chatted to. In laboratory tests, the ones kept in silence grew much slower than the ones who were talked to. It's all to do with kinetic energy.'

'In which case,' said Tansy, 'given that you talk non-stop, I should be five-foot-ten instead of the titch of Year Nine.'

'I don't think,' said her mother seriously, 'that it's very effective on humans.'

She pushed the tray of seedlings to the edge of the table and sighed.

'I wish it worked on bank notes though.' She picked up a sheaf of papers. 'Look at this lot – all bills.'

Tansy peered over her mother's shoulder.

'Mum! This one's a final demand – and this!' She waved a phone bill and an unpleasant letter from the gas board in her mother's face. 'If you don't pay, we'll get cut off. My friends would phone and find out! That would be so embarrassing!'

Her mother stood up and collected the papers together.

'Not to worry, sweetheart!' she said blithely. 'Laurence is coming over later – he'll sort it out.'

That, thought Tansy, doesn't make me feel any better at all. Laurence Murrin was her mother's totally nerdish boyfriend, who in addition to being a walking fashion disaster considered himself to be a world authority on everything and could bore for England.

Usually she could go to her boyfriend Andy's house the minute Laurence appeared, but Andy was away on a field trip and she really missed him. Especially as he couldn't provide her with an excuse for dodging the dire Laurence.

'I don't think you should let Laurence meddle with your finances,' said Tansy primly. 'It's none of his business.'

'Don't be silly, darling,' said her mother, tossing the bills on to the top of the fridge. 'He's hugely helpful – and besides, he does have one or two ideas about how we might save money.'

'*We*?' queried Tansy. 'Since I am the most financially deprived person in Year Nine, I don't see how I can be expected to cut back.'

'Well, actually darling, what Laurence was suggesting was –'

'I can guess,' interjected Tansy. 'Laurence was suggesting that I should never have new clothes, never go out to discos, never buy new make-up because the young of today don't know they are born! Yawn, yawn!'

Clarity sighed.

'Forget it,' she said. 'We'll talk about it later. Now get your things and I'll give you a lift as far as Holly's. I'm starting work on their garden today.'

Tansy frowned.

'But, Mum, it's raining,' she said.

Clarity stared out of the window in surprise.

'So it is,' she observed calmly. 'Not to worry – I can go over the design with Angela and drop off the plants. I'll just load the van.'

'I'll walk,' said Tansy hastily. 'Holly's leaving early today.' Being poor in private was one thing, advertising the fact to the entire world by driving around in her mother's disreputable pick-up with *Clarity Cultivation* scrawled on the side was quite another. She did so wish that her mother had a more elegant occupation; being a landscape gardener not only meant that she hurtled around town in faded dungarees and wellingtons smelling of compost, but also that when Tansy needed a lift anywhere, she had to share space with trays of seedlings and a couple of watering cans.

'No, darling, you have to come with me – I need you to push,' said Clarity, unhooking an ancient waterproof jacket from the back of the door and shrugging her arms into it.

'PUSH!' expostulated Tansy, running her fingers through her flyaway sandy-brown hair. 'If you think I'm pushing that heap all the way to –'

'Not all the way, silly,' said her mother, opening the back door and shoving her feet into a pair of mud-encrusted wellingtons. 'I just want a bump start down Cattle Hill – the battery's dying on me. It will only take a second.'

8.15 a.m.

After a lot of very long seconds

'Mum, this is so embarrassing!' Tansy closed her eyes and tried to blot out the sound of honking car horns behind them. 'Why can't you just get a decent car like everybody else?'

'Because decent cars, as you put it, cost money!' retorted her mother. 'It'll start up in a minute – don't panic! Now push!'

'I'm pushing as hard as I can,' Tansy shouted back,

flicking a strand of wet hair out of her eyes. 'If you didn't
have so much junk in the back it would help.'

'That's not junk!' A deep voice protested in Tansy's left
ear. 'That, unless I am very much mistaken, is a fine
specimen of *Campanula Pyramidalis*.'

A pair of immaculately gloved hands gripped the rear of
the truck.

'Allow me!'

Tansy turned to see a tall, lean man with gunmetal grey
hair eyeing the contents of the truck with the same
fascination as Tansy afforded the pin-up pages of her
magazine.

'Thanks,' she said breathlessly and then eyed him more
closely. His car coat was definitely cashmere, and the scarf
round his neck was the sort that film stars wore in the black
and white films that made her mother cry. Despite the foul
weather, he was wearing highly polished brown brogues,
and the crease in his trousers was razor sharp. He did not
look the sort of man who ever got his hands dirty, never
mind pushed pick-up trucks in the rain.

'Tansy, it's useless!' Clarity jumped out of the van and
slammed the door. 'We'll just have to ... oh!'

The guy straightened and held out his hand.

'Jonathan Pitt-Warren,' he said with a smile that
revealed two rows of perfectly symmetrical white teeth.

Clarity wiped her own hand on her dungarees and
shook his. Tansy cringed to see that she left a mud stain on
one of the fingers of his right glove.

'Clarity Meadows,' said Clarity.

'What a wonderful selection of plants you have here,
Mrs Meadows. That is a *Campanula*, isn't it?' Mr Pitt-
Warren peered closely into the back of the truck.

Clarity nodded enthusiastically.

'Yes it is, I grew it from seed for a client.'

'And in that tub – isn't that a *Lathyrus latifolia*?'

Clarity beamed.

'That's right – it's a wonderful climber, as long as you remember to –'

Tansy lost her patience. 'Mum! Could you stop playing at *Gardeners' Question Time* and move this thing? I'll be late for school.'

Mr Pitt-Warren raised his pencil-thin eyebrows.

'A teenager who actually wants to get to school? Now we really *are* talking rare specimens! Well, we mustn't keep you waiting.'

He pulled off his gloves and shoved them into his pocket.

'Now then,' he continued briskly. 'Jump leads.'

'Pardon?' said Clarity, who knew a lot about horticulture and absolutely nothing about the finer workings of the combustion engine.

'It's your battery – it must have been dying and then what with you having to use headlights and wipers in this rain, it just gave up. I'll give you a charge from my car.'

He waved a hand airily behind him to where a gleaming smoke-silver Mercedes coupé stood at the side of the road. This man, thought Tansy, with rapidly increasing interest, is seriously rich. And noted that the ungloved hands were totally ringless. Which was interesting.

'I don't think I have any jump leads,' said Clarity vaguely, glancing over her shoulder as if hoping to see a whole pile of them materialize in the middle of her watering cans.

'Then it'll have to be a bump start,' declared Mr Pitt-

Warren, apparently unfazed by Clarity's lack of organization. 'You are causing something of a traffic hazard.'

So what's new? thought Tansy, as her mother climbed back into the van.

He flexed his shoulders and heaved. Nothing happened. He tried again. Zilch.

He strode to the van door and peered through the window.

'Perhaps,' he suggested with a wry smile, 'it would help if you released the handbrake.'

'Ah,' said Clarity.

My mother, thought Tansy, is not fit to be let out on her own. Is it any wonder she couldn't remember who fathered me?

Jonathan pushed the van, which rolled obliging forwards, coughed, spluttered, coughed again and suddenly fired into life.

'Brilliant!' cried Clarity, waving an arm out the window. 'Quick, Tansy, get in before the wretched thing throws another wobbly. Thanks for your help, Mr Warren.'

'Pitt-Warren,' hissed Tansy, clambering into the van.

'Just before you go,' said Mr Pitt-Warren. 'May I have your card? I'd really like to talk to you about plants.'

Clarity frowned.

'I don't have a card – but take one of these. ' She grabbed a crumpled and rather grubby leaflet from the dashboard. Mr Pitt-Warren eyed it with interest.

'Splendid!' he said, taking a silver business-card case from his inside pocket. He removed a cream card with gold-embossed writing and handed it to Clarity.

'Here's mine – I've just acquired this new place and I do

so want to do something really different with the garden. You could be just the person I'm looking for.'

'OK,' said Clarity, slinging the card on to the dashboard. 'Must fly! Thanks again!'

And with a casual wave she rammed the car into gear and pulled out into the road.

'Mum!' exploded Tansy, snapping her seat belt in place and grabbing the card.'What do you mean – "OK, must fly"? This could be your big break – that guy's obviously mega-rich, and he'll probably spend zillions on getting his garden right and anyway, why haven't you got proper business cards instead of those grotty –'

'Tansy,' interrupted her mother, turning into Weston Way. 'I don't need business cards! I'm just a one-woman outfit, certainly not the sort that rich men employ to landscape their acres – he was just being friendly.'

'No, he wasn't – he was really impressed by your campi-whatever it is. Hey, listen to this!' She peered at the card. '*Jonathan Pitt-Warren, Director, PW Leisure Inc., The Manor, Great Massingham, Dunchestershire.*'

Clarity scrunched the gears and looked totally disinterested.

Having a mother with no ambition was such a handicap, thought Tansy.

'Don't you see,' she said, deciding to have a try at making her mother realize her potential, 'that if you got a job with Mr Pitt-Warren, we could probably afford to live somewhere like this?'

As they approached Holly's creeper-clad old house, she gazed enviously at its huge windows and sweeping gravel drive.

'I don't want to live somewhere like this,' retorted

Clarity, throwing open the van door. 'What's wrong with our dear little cottage?'

'You mean, aside from the doors that don't close and the creaking floorboards and the temperamental boiler and –'

She broke off in surprise as the front door of the Vines' house swung open and Holly, umbrella in one hand and school bag slung over her shoulder, ran down the steps.

'Hi, Mrs Meadows! Hi, Tansy!'

'Hey, how come you're still here?' demanded Tansy, jumping down from the passenger seat. 'You're supposed to be out there pulling Paul!'

'It's raining,' said Holly. 'You can't pull in the rain.'

Tansy shook her head and sighed.

'I am surrounded by defeatists,' she asserted, glaring at her mother who was unloading plants from the back of the truck. 'All looking for excuses to do nothing. You either want Paul or you don't.'

'Oh, I do,' insisted Holly. 'Don't worry, it's all in hand.'

'It is?'

Holly nodded.

'Mum's going to sort it,' she said.

'You are letting your *mother* organize your *love* life?' asked Tansy incredulously.

Admittedly, Mrs Vine was streets ahead of her own mother in the normality stakes, but this was going too far.

'Not exactly, but –'

'Where is your mum, Holly?' asked Clarity, peering over the top of a large bay tree which she was clutching to her ample bosom.

'In the kitchen with a skeleton,' said Holly with a grin.

'Fine,' said Clarity as though it was the most normal

company to keep on a Monday morning. 'You girls get off then, and I'll go round the back and find her.'

'Holly, did you say what I think you just said?' asked Tansy as they scrunched their way down the gravel drive.

'About Paul? Course I want him ...'

'No, about your mum being in the kitchen with a skeleton.'

'Yes – well, half a one. She's getting Paul's mum to sort the rest and that's how I'm getting Paul back.'

Tansy paused, stared at her friend, sighed and began walking again.

'You know,' she said, 'it's great having a friend like you.'

Holly looked chuffed.

'Thanks,' she said. 'Why especially?'

'Because it makes me realize that there are households even more nuts than my own.'

8.10 a.m.

££££

Indulging in a little vocal therapy

The trouble with dashing out of the house at half-past seven, thought Cleo, ambling down Weston Way singing under her breath, was that she had left one set of problems behind her and was immediately faced with another. Wandering around the streets with no one to talk to had meant that snatches of the dream had kept coming back to her. Half of her mind wanted to forget it, but the other half kept reaching out to the already-fading images, as if trying to recall something that would make sense of the nightmare.

She could always remember the bit of the dream when she was sitting in the car, especially the bit when she was crying and banging her fists on the window because her dad wouldn't let her see the lions. Were they at the zoo? But if they were, why could she remember ladies in long dresses sitting under a huge tree? Apart from that, the only things she could recall were the crunching noise and then the scream. And then, of course, Lettie.

Lettie lying there. White. Still. Silent.

All because of what she, Cleo, had done.

As usual the memories made her feel sick and she hadn't been able to think of it any longer, which was why she had decided to go and call for Trig, and why she had started singing as she headed for his house. She always sang when she wanted to feel brave, and lately she had been doing quite a bit of it. Her mother loved telling people that Cleo was such a happy little soul, warbling away all the time, when in fact most of her singing was done to take her mind off the fact that she *wasn't* feeling happy. But it didn't do to tell people that. It only confused them.

Singing was one of the few things she was any good at. It wasn't like maths or French, where you had to struggle to understand theorems and grammar; you didn't have to make a fool of yourself standing up in class to read French prose and getting the accent all wrong. When she sang in the choir, she could forget she was fat, forget she was thick and even daydream that she was a famous opera singer, standing on the stage at the Royal Opera House, while the audience cheered and stamped and threw bouquets of flowers at her feet.

Of course that was a pretty stupid daydream, she thought now, especially for someone who hated being looked at and always hid behind Karina Fordyce in the choir. Karina sang all the solos; Karina was tall and slim and had what Miss Saffrey called stage presence; Karina was the main reason that West Green had made it to the finals for the very first time.

Cleo gave a little skip of excitement. She was really looking forward to Saturday. Six schools were in the finals and West Green were the hosts. She wondered what they would sing – all the finalists had to come up with a new song, something they hadn't sung in any of the qualifying competitions. Miss Saffrey was very into Gilbert and Sullivan and Irish folk tunes, but Cleo secretly yearned to do a gospel song.

'*Green trees are bending, poor sinner stands a tremblin', The trumpet sounds within-a my soul, ol, ol ...*' she trilled, pacing along the pavement to the beat.

Now that would be a really cool number to do and way different from anything the other schools were likely to come up with. She'd asked Miss Saffrey if they could sing it last term, but of course, Saffers was too set in her ways to take it on board.

'*I ain't got long to stay here ...*'

Her voice strengthened as she got into the music.

She felt better. She wasn't going to waste any more time worrying about stupid dreams. She was going to concentrate all her efforts on enjoying the week and trying to get a bit more of Trig's attention. She half-closed her eyes, puckered her lips and practised looking sultry.

8.20 a.m.

For the first time in ages, Jade Williams felt good. This sense of well-being had a great deal to do with the fact that she was walking to school with Scott Hamill's arm wrapped firmly round her waist, and he had just kissed her in full view of Ella 'I Love Myself To Pieces' Hankinson, who was still miffed that he had ditched her for Jade.

Perhaps, Jade thought, a thrill running through her body as Scott's fingers tightened round her waist, things were finally beginning to get better. After her mum and dad had died, she had believed she could never be happy again. Even after she and Scott had got things together, it hadn't been plain sailing – they had even split up when Scott accused Jade of being too snooty to fit in with his huge, and very noisy, family. But they had sorted all that out now and she was determined that they weren't going to have any more misunderstandings.

'I'm glad we're still together,' said Jade, squeezing Scott's hand.

'Me too,' said Scott. 'I couldn't do with losing any more mates.'

Jade frowned.

'What do you mean?' she asked.

Scott shrugged. 'Trig's been really off lately,' he said. 'Hardly speaks and never comes round to my place any more.' He sighed.

'Do you reckon my family put him off? I mean, I know they're a bit – well, loud.'

Jade shook her head.

'Of course not,' she said. 'And talking of your family, I

guess it's time I got to know them better. Shall I come round at the weekend?'

Scott turned to her and grinned.

'That would be ace,' he said. 'You know what?'

'What?' asked Jade, hoping he wasn't going to suggest that a clutch of his cousins joined in as well.

'I love you.'

Jade's kneecaps turned to water and she suddenly felt as if she could take on the entire population of Dunchester without turning a hair.

8.45 a.m.

A not-so-boring start to the week

'Here we go again,' said Holly as she and Tansy crossed over the road to the school gates. 'Whoever thought of having double Geography first thing on a Monday must have had a very sick mind indeed ... Hey! What's with the crowd?'

The pavement was full of chattering, gesticulating West Greeners, filing slowly through the gates while Mr Grubb and Miss Saffrey stood, waving their arms and looking important.

'Just get to your classrooms and carry on as normal!' Beetle's voice resounded over their heads. 'The police are on their way.'

'Police?' said Tansy and Holly in unison.

They pushed their way through the gates and stopped still in amazement.

Three of the five huge plate-glass windows of the

assembly hall had been shattered. Great slivers of glass lay around the yard, and painted on the wall by the main door in lurid pink paint was a skull and crossbones and a few words that Mr Halfpenny, the school caretaker, was rapidly painting out with whitewash.

'What's happened?' Tansy asked Mr Grubb.

'Vandals,' said Mr Grubb through clenched teeth. 'Degenerates, imbeciles, irresponsible –'

Miss Saffrey lay a restraining hand on his arm as his face turned an alarming shade of deep puce.

'That's horrendous!' said Tansy in disgust.

'Now, just hurry along to Registration. There will be a special assembly in the gym and lessons will be starting late today.'

Holly eyed Tansy.

'On the other hand,' she said, 'every cloud has a silver lining.'

8.50 a.m.

In the locker room with a lot of hair gel

Jade stood in front of the locker-room mirror, doing her usual pre-lessons battle with her hair. It was a war she was destined to lose. She wished she had never had it all cut off; never listened when her cousin Allegra, with whom she had the misfortune to live and who had all the charm of an irate tarantula, told her how babyish she looked. Right now, she thought, babyish would be preferable to this angry hedgehog.

She tugged at a tuft of hair in disgust.

'It is growing, you know!'

Jade turned round to see Cleo smiling wanly at her. She looked even paler than usual and there were dark circles under her hazel eyes.

'I wish!' Jade hurled her hairbrush in her locker and slammed the door shut. 'Good weekend?'

'Yes, great, thanks!'

Jade wasn't fooled. That was everyone's standard Monday morning reply. If you didn't have a good weekend, it was sure evidence that you led a really sad life.

'You look awful,' she said frankly. 'Is something wrong? You haven't had a bust-up with Trig?'

'No, of course not,' said Cleo with a toss of her head. 'I'm fine – late night, that's all.'

'That's OK then,' said Jade, knowing full well it wasn't.

Nothing, thought Cleo, is OK. Nothing at all.

8.52 a.m.

Not so cool

'Hi, Trig!' Cleo pushed open the door of her classroom and tried to sound upbeat and alluring.

'Oh, hi!' Trig glanced in her direction and then buried his nose back in his book. Her heart sank. He was going off her. She just knew it.

'Year Nine, will you all settle down, please?' Miss Partridge clapped her hands in a particularly officious manner. 'Mr Boardman has popped in for a brief word.'

She smiled sweetly as the headmaster strode to the front of the room, and then she simpered into her seat.

'A word?' whispered Tansy, sidling up to Cleo who was staring miserably at Trig. 'The day Mr Boardman manages to say anything in less than ten boring paragraphs, I'll eat my hat.'

'I guess,' said Holly, sliding into a seat beside her, 'that we are going to get the "I am deeply distressed" speech.'

'I am,' said Mr Boardman, hooking his thumbs under his armpits and rocking backwards and forwards, 'deeply distressed.'

'Told you,' said Holly.

'You will all have seen the results of the deplorable act of vandalism which has been committed on our building,' he intoned. 'An act that is even more lamentable since it puts paid to this school hosting the finals of *In Voice*.'

A murmur rippled through the room.

'Not only are the windows smashed, but paint has been hurled over the floor and walls,' he said gravely. 'We are lucky that a passing motorist spotted what was going on and dialled 999.'

Cleo jumped.

'*Dial 999, dial 999.*' That's what that voice had said in the dream. '*999, call 999.*' Whose voice was it? She closed her eyes and tried to hear it again.

'Cleo,' whispered Holly. 'Are you OK? You've gone all pale.'

Cleo shook herself and nodded

'Fine, just tired – late night,' she said weakly.

Dial 999. That's it. There had been an ambulance. And a tall man saying – what was it he said?

'*Is this the culprit?*'

And he had been looking at her.

She didn't notice everyone stare as she stood up and walked out of the room. In fact, she didn't really realize that she had done so until she found herself in the corridor.

The culprit. The culprit.

She leaned against the wall. Memories of the dream were fading again but it didn't matter. Because now she knew for sure. It had all been her fault.

'Cleo, are you all right? Are you ill?'

Miss Partridge hovered at her side anxiously.

'No, no I'm fine, I'm sorry,' she gulped. 'I just felt a bit faint, that's all.'

'Well, take it quietly, dear,' said her teacher anxiously. 'Would you like me to phone your mother and have you sent home?'

'No!' said Cleo urgently. Right now home was the last place she wanted to go. What would be the point? No one would tell her what she most wanted to know.

At least here, she could go on pretending. If she tried hard enough.

10.30 a.m.

In Geography, not paying attention to the industry of the Ruhr

Cleo sat at the back of the classroom staring at the back of Trig's head. He was so lovely. And he was going to dump her. She just knew he was.

He couldn't even be bothered to talk to her these days. She thought she might just curl up and die.

'Cleopatra Greenway!' Mr Grubb's voice interrupted

her thoughts. 'I hardly think your current grades in Geography allow for you to schedule day dreaming in your timetable.'

The class tittered.

'For the second time of asking, what are the principal industries of the Ruhr valley?'

Holly mouthed something incomprehensible at her.

'I am waiting,' intoned Mr Grubb.

Something inside Cleo snapped.

'Who cares?' she said.

11.00 a.m.

In the school yard having a break

'Well, I don't think it's funny!' Jade flung her biscuit wrapper into the bin, and bit into the wafer. 'It's just not like Cleo to behave like that – and she looks dreadful. I guess something's really wrong.'

Holly tried to keep a straight face.

'It's just that Beetle's face was such a picture,' she said. 'He could hardly bring himself to say "Take detention", he was so gobsmacked.'

'I reckon it's good,' said Tansy, 'that she is developing attitude at last – and not before time.'

'Where is Cleo, anyway?' said Holly, looking round the school yard.

'Getting a lecture from Beetle, probably,' said Jade.

'Or smooching with Trig,' added Tansy.

The bell rang. The three girls headed off for their various lessons.

And in the end cubicle in the girls' toilets, Cleo sat with her head in her hands and sobbed as if her heart would break.

12.30 p.m.

In the cafeteria

He was there, at the corner table, scribbling on a piece of file paper. Cleo drummed her foot impatiently, willing the queue at the serving counter to move a little quicker.

'What are you having, dear?'

'Soup and a roll, please,' gabbled Cleo, not taking her eyes off Trig. She would really have liked beef stew but that queue was even longer. She grabbed a tray and snatched some cutlery.

She moved so fast towards Trig's table that tomato soup slopped down her skirt, but she didn't care.

'Hi!' she said, dumping the tray next to Trig. 'What are you doing?'

She peered over his shoulder at the sheet of paper.

'Nothing!' Trig grabbed the paper and thrust it into his pocket.

'Is it homework?'

'No – yes, yes. I'm late with an assigment. Anyway, got to dash. Catch you later.'

And with that he was gone.

It wasn't homework, thought Cleo miserably. If it had been, he wouldn't have been in such a hurry to hide it.

It was a letter. I bet it was a letter. To another girl.

He doesn't love me any more.

She pushed her bowl to one side. She was too miserable to eat a thing, least of all school soup.

1.00 p.m.

Choir practice

Miss Saffrey tapped her baton on the lectern and hitched her ample bosom into place.

'Now, choir,' she boomed, 'we face a dilemma. Not only has a new venue to be found for the finals, but poor little Karina is down with glandular fever and cannot sing the solos.'

A murmur rippled round the assembled singers. Everyone knew that Karina was Miss Saffrey's favourite, but poor and little she wasn't.

'But we must strive ever onward and upward!' she beamed. Miss Saffrey was the sort of woman who was always first with the tea urn in a crisis. 'And so Cleo Greenway will take over as soloist.'

Cleo, who had been watching Trig out of the corner of her eye and wishing that the boys stood near the sopranos, nearly fell off the platform.

'Well done!' whispered Jade, who was standing behind her.

'But I can't!' Cleo gasped. 'Miss Saffrey, I can't.'

'Oh, don't be so ridiculous, Cleopatra!' retorted Miss Saffrey. 'You have a delightful voice, an excellent range ...'

'... and all the best singers are fat!' someone whispered two rows behind Cleo.

Cleo felt her face burn. That settled it. OK, maybe she

could sing the notes; but as soon as the spotlight fell on her, everyone would titter and she wouldn't know where to look and ...

'Please, Miss Saffrey ...'

'Enough!' said Miss Saffrey, flicking over the pages. 'Oliver Pritchard will, of course, take the alto solos.'

'Surprise, surprise,' muttered Jade. Oliver was one of those guys who was good at absolutely everything and had a body to die for as an added bonus. And sadly, more interest in computers and advanced physics than girls.

'Right,' Miss Saffrey continued. 'For the finals, I have selected something rather different – a real rouser to make everyone sit up and take notice of West Green. It's on your yellow sheets – a gospel song which Cleo brought to my attention. "Steal Away".'

Cleo's heart lifted. She'd chosen it. Her favourite song. Perhaps she could do it. Perhaps it was an omen. After all, hadn't she vowed that she was going to change? To put the old timid Cleo behind her? This was her chance to prove it.

Her family would be stunned.

Trig would see she was a winner.

As the music struck up, she felt her shoulders drop and her lungs fill. She began to sing.

4.20 p.m.

Home to the mad house

Cleo rammed her key into the front door and stepped into the hall.

'Darling! There you are – perfect timing!' Her mother

was standing in front of the hall mirror, spraying clouds of hair lacquer in all directions. 'Now look, sweetheart, I've got to dash – my sun bed session.'

'Mum, sun beds are bad for you ...'

'Oh darling, you are a worrier! Got to look glammy for the advert, haven't I? Anyway, sweetheart, I want you to fetch Lettie from swimming at five-thirty, and then get her tea – oh, and see what's wrong with Portia. She's come home in a mood.'

'So what's new?' asked Cleo. 'Mum, guess what? I got picked for –'

'Oh, and by the way, angel,' interrupted her mother, grabbing her bag, 'I'm going straight on to my drama society meeting, so I won't be back till late. Make sure Lettie gets to bed on time, will you? And see if you can find Peaseblossom. The wretched cat's gone walkabout again.'

'Perhaps,' said Cleo, 'you'd like me to clean the windows, mow the lawn and bring about a lasting peace in Northern Ireland while I'm about it?'

Her mother pulled a face and opened the front door.

'Mum, before you go, about the festival –'

'Lovely, darling, I'm sure it will be great fun,' chirped her mother. 'Now remember what I said – I know I can rely on you. Ciao!'

And with that the door slammed.

Oh great! thought Cleo. That's all I'm good for, is it? Fetching, carrying and cooking food? Why can't you rely on Portia for a change?

'I hate you, Russell!' her elder sister's voice ricocheted down the stairs. 'I hope you rot in hell for a zillion years! I don't ever, ever want to speak to you again as long as I live!'

Portia's voice rose to a crescendo. There was a crash as the upstairs phone extension fell to the floor, followed by a high-pitched wail and the slamming of the bathroom door.

Then again, thought Cleo with a sigh, perhaps not.

4.35 p.m.

Sugar! thought Tansy, barging through the back gate and squeezing past the car that was parked next to her mother's van. *He's* here.

One of the disadvantages of her mum's boyfriend working for the Schools' Library Service was that he was always dropping in en route to and from delivering books all over the county. That wouldn't have mattered too much had her mother been able to behave like a responsible adult, but whenever Laurence turned up she went all gooey and stupid and kept kissing his nose and calling him Laurieloo, which was enough to bring on a severe case of terminal nausea.

'So you see, that way it works out beautifully!' Laurence's voice had a triumphant edge to it.

Tansy's heart sank. Not only was he here, but spread out over the kitchen table were bills and invoices and her mother's piteous attempts at a cash flow.

'It really is the simplest solution,' she heard him say as she shut the back door with a bang and headed straight for the fridge.

'Tansy, darling, you're back!' Her mother jumped up from the table with obvious relief. 'Say hello to Laurence.'

'Hello, Laurence,' said Tansy, without taking her eyes off the cheese she was hacking with a knife.

'I'll leave you in peace,' Laurence said to Clarity, picking up a sheaf of papers and shuffling them into a pile. 'I expect you'll want to put Tansy in the picture as soon as possible.'

Tansy looked up in surprise.

'What picture?' she demanded.

Clarity hesitated.

'It is an awfully big step, Laurence ...'

'It's the only step that makes any sense,' declared Laurence decisively, kissing the top of Clarity's head. 'Anyway, flowerpetal, I must dash.'

Flowerpetal? thought Tansy. Oh yuck!

'What,' she asked as Laurence backed his car out of the gate, 'was that all about? More cutbacks? More of your economy suppers?'

Tansy's mother was inclined to pick strange things in hedgerows and make them into soup when the bank manager got unpleasant.

'No, darling,' said Clarity. 'Nothing like that. Laurence has suggested that we should sell up.'

Tansy's eyes widened.

'Sell up? And get a decent house? With fitted carpets?'

This was more like it. Maybe the man did have a grain of intelligence after all.

'Not exactly,' said her mother, not meeting Tansy's eyes. 'Laurence wants us to move in with him.'

4.45 p.m.

Mother on the fringe of lunacy

Holly let herself in the front door, shrugged off her jacket

46

and ran through to the kitchen.

Her mother was standing at the kitchen sink pouring blackcurrant cordial into a length of plastic tubing.

'Hi, Mum, did you do it?'

'Hello, darling – well, I'm getting there.' She pinched the end of the tube and held it up to the light. 'Awfully effective, don't you think?'

'Effective for what?'

'As a blood vessel!' exclaimed her mother triumphantly.

'Mum,' said Holly patiently, 'if you are still on about this skeleton nonsense, I should point out that skeletons don't have blood vessels. They're dead.'

'I know that, silly!' cried her mother. 'This is for the banner – "The lifeblood is being sucked out of Dunchester General". And then we drip the cordial out of the tube as we march on the hospital. Magic, don't you think?'

'Manic, more like,' said Holly. 'Anyway, what did Paul's mum say? You didn't mention me, did you? What did you talk about? Does she like me?'

Holly's mother dumped her invention into the sink, wiped her hands on a tea towel and sat down at the table.

'It would hardly have been possible to find out if she liked you if I wasn't permitted to mention your name,' she reasoned. 'Besides, I didn't go.'

'DIDN'T GO!' expostulated Holly. 'What do you mean, you didn't go!'

'Well, first of all Clarity came and we had such fun planning the rockery – grape hyacinths, we thought, and a little rippling fountain – and then I had to meet Dilys Pugh, you know, nice woman, red hair, organizes the mobile trolley at the hospital ...'

'Never mind trolleys,' retorted Holly impatiently.

'Although if she's a friend of yours, she's probably off hers. You said you were going to see Mrs Bennett about the skeleton. It's important, Mum!'

Her mother looked surprised.

'You know, darling, I think it's lovely that you are so fired up about this hospital thing – maybe we could work on it together.'

'MUM! Just get over to Mrs Bennett's and sort it out!' demanded Holly. 'Now!'

Angela held up her hands in mock surrender.

'OK, OK, I'm going.'

The telephone on the kitchen wall shrilled.

'I'll get it,' said Holly. 'It's bound to be for me anyway. Now go!'

She picked up the receiver.

'Dunchester eight-six-four-five ... oh, hi, Tansy!'

She waved her mother out of the back door.

'Listen,' said Tansy urgently, 'something mega-awful has happened and you've got to help me. I think my mother is going mad.'

'Going? At least you're in with a chance then,' sighed Holly. 'Mine's already gone stir crazy. What's up?'

Tansy told her.

'This,' agreed Holly, 'is serious. You'll have to speak to her, make her see sense. Be firm. Make her listen.'

'Since when,' asked Tansy with a sigh, 'did any of that work on a mother?'

'There is,' said Holly, 'always a first time.'

5.30 p.m.

Sisterly angst

Cleo pushed her way through the revolving doors into West Green Leisure Pool. Lettie was waiting by the drinks machine and it was obvious she had been crying.

'Hey, Lettie, what's the matter?' Cleo put an arm round her shoulder.

She found her sister a pain most of the time, but she hated to see anyone unhappy.

'Nothing,' said Lettie.

Cleo eyed her closely.

'Your hair's dry,' she said. 'And so is your towel. You didn't swim, did you?'

Lettie burst into tears.

'Hey, it's OK,' said Cleo, ushering her out into the street, 'it's no big deal. But you're a brill swimmer – what happened?'

'Same as always,' retorted Lettie. 'People look.'

Cleo bit her lip.

'At your leg?'

Lettie nodded.

'At the scars,' she whispered.

'*Scarred for life, she'll be scarred for life.*' An image of the dream flashed into her mind and straight out again.

'And they call me Crab Foot,' she gulped. 'Why did it have to happen? Why does it have to be me that has a funny-shaped foot? I want to wear mini skirts, not trousers all the time.'

The usual guilt swamped Cleo.

'Do you remember the accident?' she asked softly. 'I

mean, everything that happened?'

Lettie shook her head.

'No. Mum said a car knocked me down and ran over my leg. I remember the car, it was white ...

An image of the big white car with leather seats and a clock on the dashboard flashed through Cleo's mind. She knew that car so well. The car of her nightmare.

'And then I remember a big bed and getting a doll that wet itself,' she said. 'And one day I asked where you were and Mum said you wouldn't be coming to see me. I was cross.'

'She said that?'

Lettie nodded.

'Why didn't you come?'

'I can't remember,' said Cleo. 'I only wish I could.'

6.45 p.m.

At supper – not happy

'I don't believe you are saying all this!' Tansy pushed her plate to one side and glared at her mother. 'How can you even *think* about moving in with that jerk!'

She grabbed her glass of lemonade and took a big gulp to stop herself from crying.

'He is not a jerk!' said Clarity. 'I'm very fond of him.'

'Can't you be fond of him in your own home?'

'Think of all the money it will save,' ventured Clarity. 'It's a real struggle, you know, making ends meet on my money. And considering how much time Laurence and I spend together, what's the point of heating two houses, paying two mortgages ... it does make sense.'

'Oh, does it?' retorted Tansy. 'And I suppose my feelings don't count for anything?'

'Of course they do, sweetheart,' said her mother. 'I thought you'd like the idea of a bigger house – it's in Oak Hill, you know ...'

'I don't care if it's in the grounds of Buckingham Palace,' shouted Tansy. 'This is our home.'

Clarity sighed.

'This morning,' she said, 'you hadn't a good word to say for the cottage. This morning you wanted me to aim high. Well, I'm aiming.'

'Well, Laurence Murrin is the wrong target! Mum, you can't do this. I'll do a paper round. I'll give up my magazines. I'll –'

Her mum laid a hand on her arm.

'I've told Laurence I won't make a decision until the end of the week,' she assured her. 'I won't rush into anything – I'm not completely stupid.'

You could, thought Tansy, stomping upstairs to do her homework, have fooled me.

8.00 p.m.

£££

Fatherly faux pas

Please be there, prayed Cleo silently, pressing the receiver to her ear. Please, Dad, be there.

'Max Greenway!' Cleo's heart lifted at the sound of her father's voice.

'Hi, Dad, it's me – Cleo!'

'Cleo darling, how lovely – and I'm so pleased you've phoned. I've got some news.'

'Me too,' said Cleo excitedly. 'You go first.'

'I'm going to be a father!' The pride in Max's voice was almost tangible over the phone.

'But you are a father,' reasoned Cleo. 'You – oh! You mean, Fleur ...'

'Yes, darling – Fleur's pregnant! And guess what? She's having twins!'

Cleo opened her mouth to say something but no sound would come out. There was a tight lump where her tonsils would have been if she had still had them and her legs suddenly felt shaky.

'Cleo? Cleo, you are pleased, aren't you? I wanted to tell you first because you're the rational one – no tantrums from my sensible Cleo, eh?' He laughed nervously.

I don't feel sensible or rational, she wanted to shout. And no, I am not pleased. Ever since you went, I dreamed that you'd miss Mum so much that you'd come back and send Roy packing and we'd all be a happy family again, and now I know that will never happen.

'Yes, Dad, it's great,' she said flatly.

'They're due in April,' he said, 'and we both want boys. I've done the girls bit.'

Oh terrific, thought Cleo. Thanks a heap.

'Now, darling, what's your news?'

'I've been chosen to sing the solos at the In Voice finals on Saturday,' she said, all her excitement ebbing in the light of her father's revelation.

'Splendid! I always knew your voice was special. Remember when you used to sit on my knee and sing "Waltzing Matilda" to me?'

Cleo smiled despite herself.

'Except I kept saying "Walking My Hilda",' she laughed. 'Dad, you will come up for the finals, won't you? Please.'

There was a lengthy pause.

'Is your mother going?'

Here we go again, thought Cleo. It's pathetic that they won't even sit in the same room together. I've had it up to here with all this. The new go-for-it Cleo wouldn't stand for it.

'No,' she lied. 'She will be filming for a TV advert. And Roy's playing in a golf tournament,' she invented, before the next inevitable question.

'Wonderful!' enthused her father. 'Then you can count on us being there. Where is it?'

Cleo told him about the vandalism.

'So I'll call you as soon as I know the venue, OK?'

'Right you are, darling,' he said. 'And you will tell your mother and the other two about the babies, won't you?'

If I must, thought Cleo.

'Must dash now – going house hunting. Can't bring twins up on a barge, you know.'

'Dad – about houses, Roy says ...'

'What Roy says about anything is unlikely to be worth running up a phone bill over. Must go, honey.'

And with that the phone went dead.

TUESDAY

4.00 a.m.

That dream again

The car was moving. Daddy wasn't in it. Just Cleo.
'I'm driving,' she called. Daddy's face at the window.
Daddy screaming. Daddies don't scream. Not ever.
'Lettie, Lettie!' Daddy sobbing.
Get up, Lettie.
'How could Cleo have done that?'

'Aaaah! No, no, Dad!' Cleo sat bolt upright in bed, perspiration pouring down her neck and her heart racing so fast she could hardly breathe. Forget it, forget it. Put the light on. No, remember. You must remember.

Dad had been there. Dad had got her out of the car. The car had been moving and no one had been in it. No one but Cleo. She had done it. She had knocked Lettie down.

Cleo's hands were shaking as she lifted her glass of water to her lips. It must have been her fault that the car moved on its own. She must have let the brake off. Everyone always said there had been some silly accident, and that no one was to blame. But of course they would say that, wouldn't they? She knew they did blame her; that was why it was always Cleo who had to fit in with everyone else, Cleo who had to make sure everyone else was happy.

And, of course, that was why Dad had left. Because he couldn't bear, day after day, to see her face, knowing that because of her Lettie was disabled. It all made sense now. And that was why Dad wanted the babies to be boys.

Because if they were boys there was no chance they would remind him of her.

She rolled over on to her stomach, stuffed a handkerchief into her mouth and sobbed.

7.05 a.m.

Suffering the effects of a broken heart

Holly stood in the bathroom, pressing a cold face flannel to her eyes in the hope that the puffiness that had appeared after so much crying wouldn't show by the time she got to school.

'You've been ages!' Holly had exclaimed the evening before, when her mother returned from Paul's house, with flushed cheeks and wearing the sort of silly grin that suggested it wasn't tea she had been drinking. 'So what happened?'

Her mother had hugged her.

'Stupendous news!' she enthused. 'Not only will Deannie make the skeleton, but she's coming on the protest with me! She's up in arms!'

'So,' Holly had said, studying her fingernails and trying to look disinterested, 'was Paul there?'

'Paul? Oh, no, dear, Deannie was saying he'd gone out with Amy – that's the young girl who –'

'What do you mean gone out? Gone out where?'

Holly's mother had been taken aback.

'Well, how should I know? I didn't ask for a detailed itinerary. Deannie just said that it was such a relief to her that Paul got on like a house on fire with Amy because –'

'Oh, did she? Did she really? And I suppose you just sat there and said nothing? Well, thanks a bunch.'

And with that she had stormed upstairs and refused to go down all evening.

She had hardly slept a wink. Every time she nodded off she dreamed of Paul kissing Amy and woke up just before she closed her hands round that porcelain throat. And how dare Paul's mum be relieved that he was going out with someone other than Holly?

There had to be a way to get him back. There had to be. Because if she didn't, she would almost certainly die.

7.45 a.m.

Insane mothers and upmarket visitors

'... and you wouldn't like his house, Mum – you know you hate modern boxes, and besides, you're not married!'

Tansy paused in her lecture about Laurence's

interfering ways, dumped her cereal bowl in to the sink and turned on the tap.

'Oh, darling, loads of people live together these days, and besides –'

'Well, no mother of mine is going to!' stormed Tansy, squirting washing-up liquid over a large area. 'Honestly, Mum, the newspapers keep blaming teenagers for declining standards, when all the time it's down to mothers like you.'

'Yes, well, it would be, wouldn't it?' commented Clarity dryly. 'Anyway, what is it you lot keep saying? "It's my life"? Well, this is mine.'

Tansy was about to protest when the doorbell rang.

'Get that, will you?' ordered Clarity. 'I've got to load the van.'

Tansy sighed deeply, padded through the sitting room, and wrenched open the front door. And gasped.

Standing on the step, wearing what was definitely Italian knitwear and with a slate-grey suede jacket slung casually over his shoulders, was Jonathan Pitt-Warren.

'I am sorry to call at such an early hour,' he said, 'but I wonder if I could possibly have a word with your mother.'

'Of course,' said Tansy, waving him in. 'I'll get her. Have a seat – no, not that one, the springs have gone and you get wire up your b ... it's uncomfortable.'

She pointed him to the one decent chair in the room and scooted off to retrieve her mother from the yard.

'It's Mr Pitt-Warren,' she hissed, 'and he wants to see you. Now.'

Clarity straightened and glanced at her watch.

'But I'm just off to Angela's,' she said. 'Tell him to call back later.'

'MUM!' Tansy exclaimed. 'You are unreal. Do you think Richard Branson got rich by telling people to come back later? Now get in there and talk to him. I'll load the van.'

Her mother stomped none too graciously back into the house. He has to want her to work for him, thought Tansy. No one comes round at eight in the morning if it's not important. She lugged a couple of baby conifers to the van, hurled a few seed trays in the back and crept back into the house.

'... and, of course, then there is the water garden,' she heard Jonathan explain. 'It's been allowed to go to rack and ruin but I'm sure there is potential.'

Tansy strolled into the sitting room and Jonathan looked up.

'I'm trying to persuade your mother to take on my patch,' he said. 'I think she's wavering.'

'Oh, she'd love to do it, wouldn't you, Mum?' said Tansy firmly. 'She's ever so good with water gardens.'

'Tansy, I have never –'

'Tell you what,' said Mr Pitt-Warren eagerly. 'How about we go out to dinner tonight and we talk it all through?'

He leaned towards Clarity and a whiff of expensive aftershave assailed Tansy's nostrils.

'Oh no, I couldn't, you see, I've already got –'

'Great, she'd love it!' said Tansy. 'She doesn't get out much – she's so dedicated to her work, you see!'

Clarity appeared to have lost the power of speech.

'I'll show you out, Mr Pitt-Warren ...' said Tansy.

'Jonathan, please.'

'Jonathan,' Tansy corrected herself. 'What time will you pick Mum up? Eight p.m.? Brill – I'm so pleased she's going to work for you. You won't find anyone better!'

She shut the door and grabbed her school bag.

'Tansy! How dare you take over like that? How dare you organize my life! And what am I going to tell Laurence about this dinner date?'

Oh good, so she is going, thought Tansy.

'How about telling him to stuff –'

'Tansy!'

'Bye, Mum!'

7.55 a.m.

Don't shoot the messenger!

'I spoke to Dad last night,' ventured Cleo at breakfast. It was one of those rare days when every member of the family was in the kitchen at the same time and she reckoned there was safety in numbers. 'There's something he wanted me to tell you all.'

How do I put this? she asked herself.

'The thing is,' she began, 'Fleur –'

'Don't speak that woman's name in this house!' exclaimed her mother. 'Whatever possessed him to take off with that bimbo, I shall never know!'

'Did your father say anything about a cheque?' demanded Roy, who was sitting at the table eyeing a phone bill with intense displeasure.

'No, but –'

'Typical!' Roy thumped a fist on the table.

'Why didn't you let me talk to him?' demanded Lettie, ladling honey on to a piece of toast.

'Why would you want to?' retorted Portia.

'JUST SHUT IT, ALL OF YOU!' Cleo yelled. 'Dad rang to say that Fl– that they are expecting twins.'

There was a stunned silence. No one moved.

'In April. They want boys.'

Suddenly the whole kitchen was in uproar. Diana hurled her piece of toast into the air and it fell, marmalade side down, on Roy's trousers.

'It's too cruel, too too cruel to bear!' She jumped up and flounced out the kitchen.

Roy followed, muttering about temperamental bloody women and the cost of dry cleaning.

'That is positively and utterly disgusting!' shouted Portia, pushing back her chair and jumping up. 'At his age – it's sordid!'

And she too stormed out of the room.

Lettie sat silently, her shoulders shaking.

'Hey, Lettie – it's OK,' said Cleo.

'Why does he want more babies?' she cried.

Cleo frowned.

'I guess Fleur wants some of her own,' she volunteered.

'He used to say I was his baby. Now he wants new ones. One's that aren't ugly and run crooked.'

She may never walk without a limp.

Another forgotten echo of her dream stabbed her consciousness.

'I wish he loved me, Cleo,' she whispered.

'He does, honestly he does.'

Lettie shook her head.

'Then why did he go away and leave us?'

Because of me. Because he couldn't bear to look at me after what I'd done to you.

'Come on, Lets, we've got to get to school.'

It wasn't until she was on the way to school that she realized she still hadn't had time to tell her family about being picked as soloist.

It could wait. She had a feeling that no one would care that much anyway.

8.10 a.m.

Wandering to school

'So what I thought was, that if she works for Jonathan, and they're on top of one another day after day, well, they might get together and then we wouldn't have to move in with the loopy Laurence.'

Tansy turned enthusiastically to Holly as they walked to school.

'Have you heard a word I've been saying?' she demanded.

Holly sighed.

'Sorry,' she said. 'It's Paul.'

'Oh yes,' said Tansy. 'I forgot to ask – did you find out anything?'

'Too much,' said Holly morosely. 'Paul's going out with that girl. She's called Amy and his mother approves of her.'

'Oh, that's OK then,' said Tansy contentedly.

'What do you mean, that's OK?' snapped Holly. 'You're supposed to be my friend, my suffering is supposed to be your suffering ...'

'What I mean,' said Tansy patiently, 'is that if his mum approves, he won't be with her for long, will he? Parents never approve of anyone halfway sassy.'

Holly looked thoughtful.

'Do you think so?'

'Sure of it,' said Tansy. 'It's only a matter of time.'

9.15 a.m.

£££

Preparing to be thrilled

'I have,' declared Mr Boardman, the headmaster, smiling benignly at the kids who were crammed into the cafeteria for a makeshift assembly, 'some positively thrilling news.'

Bearing in mind that Plank got excited about new blinds at the science block windows, no one showed too much interest.

'We have a venue for the *In Voice* finals,' he declared. 'And not just any venue, either. The choirs will all have the huge honour of singing at Great Massingham Manor!'

A murmur rippled round the room.

'Great Massingham Manor! That's where Mr Pitt-Warren lives!' Tansy exclaimed, nudging Holly. 'You know, the guy I was telling you about?'

Holly looked impressed.

'We have been given permission to use the magnificent banqueting hall with its historic minstrels' gallery. It is a great opportunity for you all.'

Never mind the rest of them, thought Tansy, her brain racing, this could be my big chance. Fate had thrown Jonathan in their path and now it was up to her to make sure that her mother didn't blow it. Because If Mr P-W could fall madly in love with her mum, they would be spared the dreaded Laurence and she would be on the road to the fame and fortune she so passionately believed was hers by right.

'This Pitt chap must be rolling in it,' muttered Holly, as Plank droned on.

'He is,' agreed Tansy. And I intend to have some of it. I wasn't born to be poor, she thought. And if I have anything to do with it, I won't be for very much longer.

Tansy Meadows of Great Massingham Manor was just the sort of entrée she needed into high society.

10.15 a.m.

In French – making decision

It was while she was grappling with her French translation and wondering why foreigners chose to use ten words when two would suffice, that Holly decided she was being too soft. She had to confront Paul, ask him what he thought he was doing, hanging out with some other girl, when he was supposed to be her boyfriend.

Assertiveness, that's what Birdie was always on about in PSE lessons. Well, assertive was what she was going to be.

Today.

11.00 a.m.

At break

'I am going to assert myself,' Holly informed Tansy over a can of cola.

'So what's new?' asked Tansy.

Charming! thought Holly.

11.15 a.m.

In Chemistry

On the other hand, maybe she should try the accommo-
dating approach. Ask Paul about the girl in a kind of 'wouldn't
it be fun to get to know her better?' sort of way.

11.20 a.m.

In Chemistry mopping up spilt acid

Shucks to that idea.

12 noon.

Still in Chemistry

Of course, she could keep Paul out of it altogether. If she
could just get the wretched girl on her own ...

12.05 p.m.

Eureka!

Now that was a good idea.

12.06 p.m.

Oh whoops!

'Holly Vine! Would you stop staring out of the window and concentrate on the important issues in life! Such as your none-too-satisfactory grades!'

There is no more important issue in life than getting Paul back.

'Sorry, Miss Bainbridge.'

Silly old bat.

1.00 p.m.

In the garden of The Cedars – wishing life were simple

Tansy's mother stuck her spade in the soil and straightened her aching back. She wondered whether she dared pop up to the house and ask Angela Vine to pay her by the day – that way, she could get some cash to settle the telephone bill before they got cut off. She was almost at her overdraft limit, not that she had dared admit that bit to Laurence. She knew he would offer to help but she didn't want him to. Not yet. Not until she had decided.

Of course, living with Larry would make life a lot easier. It made sound economic sense. But then again, it was such a huge step – she had been on her own for so many years and she didn't take kindly to being told what to do and when to do it.

But he did love her and she was almost sure she loved

him. And she certainly couldn't cope much longer on the pittance she earned.

She'd do it. She would. After all, there was more to life than feeling sick every time the postman came.

4.30 p.m.

Confrontation

Holly couldn't believe her luck. That Amy girl was there, hanging about outside Paul's front gate. She was wearing the same expensive coat and had a to-die-for velvet cloche hat pulled down over her ears. Holly had to admit that she looked a million dollars.

Holly hesitated, wondering what to do. The girl kept looking anxiously up and down the road like a lost soul. Obviously she was waiting for him. Well, she'll have a long wait, thought Holly smugly, because on Tuesdays Paul has computer club until six o'clock. Which gives me plenty of time to sort her out once and for all.

'I am Holly Vine,' she said striding up to Amy, and recalling what Miss Partridge said about establishing eye contact to give you added authority. 'And I am Paul's girlfriend.'

She tapped the girl on the shoulder and she practically jumped out of her skin. Ah, thought Holly, guilty conscience at work.

'So you might as well stop wasting your time hanging around him!'

Amy's brow furrowed into a deep frown and she shook her head furiously.

'Oh, I get it,' shouted Holly. 'You think you can take him off me. Well, you just try. How old are you anyway? Twelve? Thirteen? Do you honestly think Paul would be interested in a kid like you?'

She tried not to think of the affectionate way that Paul had gazed at the kid the week before. He was just being nice. That was all.

'Get it?' demanded Holly.

Amy's eyes suddenly filled with tears. For one instant, Holly wondered if she had gone too far. But since the kid hadn't the decency to reply, she decided she deserved all she got.

'Well?'

Amy tilted her chin defiantly, glared at Holly and then turned and marched off down the road without a word.

That told her, thought Holly. And wondered why she didn't feel better about it.

4.45 p.m.

In determined mood

A lot of people, thought Cleo, marching into the kitchen, would be surprised to find their mother standing on a chair in her bra and knickers, with a parasol in one hand and a chiffon scarf floating from the other. But then a lot of people had normal mothers. Sadly she did not.

'Mum, I need to talk to you.' She had decided on the assertive approach which *Heaven* magazine said was a sure way of commanding parental attention.

'Of course, angel – just let me work out this pose and then –'

'No, Mum. Now. It's serious.'

Immediately Diana's face creased with concern.

'What's happened, Cleo? What's wrong?'

Seeing her mother suddenly becoming all mother-like threw Cleo a little. She decided to start with the easy bit.

'I've been chosen to sing the solo on Saturday,' she said. And as she did so, a brilliant idea flew into her mind. 'You will come, won't you? Please?'

'Darling, that's wonderful! I wouldn't miss it for all the world,' her mother enthused. 'On one condition.'

Here we go, thought Cleo.

'You're not going to go and ask your father and that woman, are you?'

'No, Mum.' Well, it's not a lie; I'm not going to, because I already have.

'That's all right, then,' said her mother. 'Now darling, if you could just unhook this bra ...'

'I haven't finished, Mum.'

Diana paused

Cleo took a deep breath.

'Lettie asked me why I never went to visit her when she was in the hospital. After the accident.'

Diana drew her breath in sharply and bit her lip.

'What a funny question!' she exclaimed with false brightness.

'No, it's not funny, Mum, it's serious,' said Cleo.

Her mother swallowed.

'I remember,' she said suddenly. 'You had German measles! And of course, we couldn't risk infecting Lettie when she was so – while she was getting better, so we didn't take you.'

Cleo eyed her mother.

'But, Mum,' she said, trying to keep the wobble out of her voice, 'I've never had German measles, remember? That's why I had the jab at school last year.'

'Oh well,' said her mother impatiently. 'Chickenpox, scarlet fever, whatever – how am I expected to remember?'

To Cleo's horror, her mother's eyes filled with tears.

'It's all in the past, why rake it up?' she said. 'It doesn't do anyone any good.'

She brushed a hand across her face, and fixed a smile on her lips.

'Anyway, all's well that ends well – Lettie's fine and that's what matters.'

Yes, of course, thought Cleo. My stupid dream isn't really important. Lettie is.

'Now then,' said her mother, twirling round. 'How do you think I look? Are there any bulges?'

Cleo shook her head

'There is one thing that would make it look better though,' she said, trying to lighten the atmosphere.

'What's that, darling?' Her mother look worried.

'Clothes,' said Cleo.

5.30 p.m.

Organizing mother

'And so the finals are going to be at Great Massingham Manor!' Tansy finished triumphantly after relating the day's events to her mother.

'That huge place on the outskirts of Dunchester? So someone has bought it at last,' remarked her mother, tenderly replacing the lid on a seed propagator.

'Mum! That's where Mr Pitt-Warren lives – remember, it was on his card?'

Clarity's eyes widened.

'Good heavens,' she said. 'Was it really?'

It is amazing, thought Tansy, that my mother ever manages to grasp the essentials for everyday living, never mind convince people to employ her.

'I told you,' she said with exaggerated patience. 'Mum, you have to land this job. I mean, think how much work the garden of a place like that will need.'

Clarity's face brightened.

'Well,' she said, 'it certainly sounds an exciting project. But then ...'

Her voice trailed off.

'Then what?'

'Well, if we move in with Larry, he doesn't want me to work so much.'

'Oh doesn't he!' shouted Tansy. 'So not content with taking over your life, he's now decided he doesn't even want you to have one!'

'Tansy, it's not like that ...'

No, it certainly won't be if I have anything to do with it, she thought.

'Mum, go and have a bath. Now. And put smelly stuff in. And shave your legs.'

There were times, she thought, as her mother padded reluctantly upstairs, when being a daughter could be a very stressful experience.

7.15 p.m.

Speaking the unspeakable

'Portia?'

'What?'

'What do you remember about Lettie's accident?'

Portia paused in her application of purple mascara and peered at Cleo.

'Why do you want to know?'

So she does remember things, thought Cleo. Tread carefully.

'I can only remember bits, but you were seven at the time,' said Cleo. 'I mean, how did it all happen?'

'A car ran over her leg and –'.

'I know that!' said Cleo, taking a deep breath and wandering over to the window. 'Who was driving?'

There was a long silence.

'No one,' said Portia at last. 'She was playing, the car rolled backwards on its own, and squashed her leg.'

The view of the garden blurred. Go on, say it. You have to know. Go on, say it.

'Was anyone in the car? Anyone at all?'

There was another, even longer silence.

Cleo turned slowly and stared at her sister. Portia looked away.

Cleo said no more. She didn't need to. She had her answer. And she didn't think she could bear it.

7.45 p.m.

In disbelief

'You are not going out dressed like that, are you?' Tansy stood on the landing staring at her mother in disbelief.

'That,' said Clarity, 'is supposed to be my line. And anyway, what's wrong with it?'

'You want a list?' retorted Tansy. 'Mum, cheesecloth skirts are way out of fashion, and that shirt is ages old. And you haven't got enough make-up on. You've got to make an effort.'

'Tansy,' said her mother through gritted teeth, 'I am going out to discuss a gardening project, not to attend London Fashion Week. Anyway, Laurence says I look adorable in this outfit.'

'That,' said Tansy, 'says it all.'

8.35 p.m.

An unwanted caller

'Bother!' Tansy turned the volume down on the TV and went to answer the shrilling doorbell.

Standing on the step, clutching a bottle of wine and a large bunch of flowers, was Laurence.

'Hi, Tansy!' He made to step into the hallway. Tansy blocked his path.

'Mum in?' he frowned.

'Nope.'

'Out, is she?'

'There are only two alternatives,' said Tansy. 'In and out.'

Laurence's smile faded.

'So where is she?'

Tansy smiled sweetly.

'Dining at The Snooty Fox,' she said. 'With Jonathan. I'll tell her you called. Must dash. Bye!'

WEDNESDAY

7.45 a.m.

Mouth-watering talk

'... and then I had this amazing vanilla soufflé with raspberry coulis, and then cheese and coffee with –'

'And the job, Mum?' said Tansy impatiently. 'Did you get the job?'

'I did,' said Clarity smugly. 'Three days a week while I finish the Vines' garden and then full time till the redesigning is finished.'

Tansy leapt up and hugged her.

'That's wonderful!' she cried. 'I am so pleased for you!'

She was giving her mother a second breathstopping squeeze when the back door opened and Laurence walked in.

'Where were you last night?' he demanded. 'I take it Tansy told you I called.'

Clarity shook her head.

'Sorry. Forgot. Must dash. School.' Tansy gave her mother another quick kiss and fled.

'You didn't tell me you were going out!' Laurence's

voice followed her into the hallway.

'Do I have to tell you everything I do?' Clarity sounded aggrieved.

Go for it, Mum!

'And just who is Jonathan?'

Only the guy who is going to save us from a lifetime of you, thought Tansy.

'It was just business,' she heard her mother explain, a pleading note in her voice.

For now, thought Tansy, opening the front door. But hopefully not for long.

10.20 a.m.

In English

Dear Tansy,

I did it! I confronted that pain Amy and told her just what I thought about the way she was trying to muscle in on Paul. She left with her tail between her legs, I can tell you. This assertiveness thing that Birdie goes on about really does work.

Love, Holly

PS What's the answer to question 7?

Dear Holly,
6.3345. But what did this Amy girl say?
Love, Tansy

Dear Tansy,
Nothing. Zilch. Zippo. She just looked all pathetic and flounced off. Wet or what?

Anyway, I'm going to call on Paul tonight and be all charming to his mother. And then I intend to make sure Paul forgets that girl ever existed.

Love, Holly

1.40 p.m.

In choir practice

'Oliver dear, we shall sing the first verse and then you come in with your solo.' Miss Saffrey beamed and flicked over her music.

'I'm not doing it, Miss Saffrey.' Oliver Pritchard pulled himself up to his full height, his face flushed and fists clenched.

The choir members gasped. Miss Saffrey's chest lifted.

'What do you mean, you are not doing it?'

'I'm not singing the solo,' he said. 'I've had it with dumb festivals. You'll have to find some other sucker!'

And with that he turned and ran out of the music room.

The room exploded in uproar.

'But he's got a great voice! Why won't he? What's happened?'

'Thinks he's too good for us, I guess!'

Miss Saffrey rapped the lectern with her baton.

'Quiet!' she boomed. 'I shall sort out this ridiculous charade later. We shall take verse two and Cleo's solo.'

The murmurs went on.

'Choir,' shouted Miss Saffrey, 'sing.'

They sang.

2.00 p.m.

On a mission

'Hey, Olly, wait!' Cleo panted up the Art block stairs and drew level with Oliver.

Olly glanced at her and kept walking.

'Look,' said Cleo, 'I don't mean to pry or anything but –'

'Then don't!' retorted Oliver.

'But why won't you sing? I mean, I know it's scary –'

'Who says I'm scared?'

'Well, I guess you must be or you wouldn't have backed out. You're the best alto in the school, you've done Choirboy of the Year and everything ...'

'Yes, when I was a kid. But I'm not a kid any longer, OK?'

'Sure, I know that but look, Olly, the festival is in three days' time and you're the only one who can do it.'

'Oh I get it!' Olly stormed, so loudly that several passing Year Eights stared at him in astonishment. 'Old Saffers has sent you to butter me up. Well, it won't work. Read my lips. I am not doing it.'

Cleo had had enough.

'Look, you,' she ranted. 'I'm dead scared – and with far more cause than you. But at least I wouldn't back out at the last minute and ruin everyone's chances. You said you're not a kid. Well, you're behaving like one. Why don't you grow up!'

And with that she stormed into Ceramics, leaving Olly staring, open-mouthed, after her.

'Boys!' she spat, and let her wrath out on an unsuspecting piece of damp clay.

4.00 p.m.

Cleo ran across the school yard and caught up with Trig at the gates.

'Walking home?' she asked, her heart in her mouth.

Trig shook his head.

'Got to go to the ... into town,' he said. 'I'm catching the bus.'

'I'll come too, if you like,' suggested Cleo eagerly.

'No, don't,' replied Trig hastily. 'I'll be ages.'

'That's OK, I can ring my mum,' said Cleo.

'I said no!' Trig snapped. 'Sorry – I mean, it's really nice of you to suggest it, but I've got a load of kind of private stuff to do. I'll catch up with you tomorrow, OK?'

'OK,' said Cleo dully.

Only it wasn't.

4.30 p.m.

Seeking consolation

'Cleo, is that you?' Her mum stuck her head round the sitting-room door as Cleo let herself into the house. 'Thought you'd be later than this – you usually go round to Trig's on a Wednesday.'

Cleo's eyes filled with tears.

'Darling, what is it? What's wrong?'

'Oh, Mum!' Cleo flung herself into her mother's arms.

'Sweetheart, what's happened? Has Trig upset you?'

Cleo gulped and told her mother everything.

'So you see, I'm sure he doesn't want me, despite all the things he said,' she sobbed. 'Why does everything I do always go wrong?'

'Darling, of course it doesn't,' protested her mother. 'Look at your singing – not everyone gets chosen as soloist in a choir festival, you know. I shall be so proud.'

'Really?'

'Of course – now tell me, where is it being held? I never did ask.'

Cleo wiped her eyes on her sleeve.

'Massingham Manor,' she said, trying to smile. 'A bit more swanky than our school hall. Mum?'

Her mother was staring at her, her mouth half open.

'The finals – they're going to be at Massingham Manor?'

Cleo nodded. 'Why? What's wrong?'

'Wrong? Oh nothing, nothing at all. Now then, would you like a cup of tea? That'll make you feel better.'

All the tea in China won't make me feel better, thought Cleo. My heart is broken. For ever.

9.10 p.m.

Eavesdropping at the bathroom door

'I can't do it, Roy, I simply can't.'

Cleo paused, head wrapped turban-style in a towel, and strained her ears.

'But, Di, you have to – it's her big day,' she heard Roy protest. 'You can't let her down.'

'Roy – I am not going and that is that. It will all be too awful.'

She doesn't think I can do it, thought Cleo miserably. She thinks I'll let her down in public. She's not coming.

'And what will you say to poor Cleo?' demanded Roy.

'I'll think of some excuse,' her mother replied impatiently. 'Anyway, you can go.'

'I will, believe me,' said Roy. 'That's the very least I can do, poor kid.'

Poor kid. It will all be too awful. So much for changing into spunky Cleo that everyone respected. Some hope. Even my own mother can't say she's proud of me and mean it. She's ashamed of me, she thought. Thank goodness Dad's coming up. At least someone cares.

9.20 p.m.

More disappointment

'Hi, Dad, it's Cleo. About the choir finals ... yes, it's going to be at Massingham Manor ... Dad? Are you still there? ... Oh good. Massingham Manor – just outside Dunchester on the Kettleborough road.'

She twiddled a damp strand of hair between her fingers.

'What? But you promised – you said you and Fleur would both come ... You can't. Great, Dad. Thanks a bunch.'

She slammed the receiver down and hurled her towel across the room. She was too angry even to cry.

10.00 p.m.

Water, water everywhere

'Mum! Come quickly! Help!'

Clarity leapt up the stairs two at a time at the sound of Tansy's shrieks.

'Look!'

Tansy was standing in the middle of her bedroom floor pointing at the ceiling. A steady and increasingly rapid drip was splashing on to the bed.

'Oh no!' Clarity clamped a hand to her mouth and looked wildly round the room as if hoping that the rescue services would appear as if by magic. 'It must be that old galvanised water tank – get some towels, quickly!'

'Mum, get real! You'll be suggesting a couple of tissues next,' said Tansy. 'Don't you have to turn off the water or something?'

'I'll phone Laurence, that's what I'll do. He'll sort it.'

11.00 p.m.

Damp but relieved

'Oh, Laurence, darling, how can I thank you? You were wonderful.'

For pity's sake, the man's got a big enough ego as it is, thought Tansy, without you inflating it even further.

'That old tank must have been seeping for months,' admonished Laurence. 'I told you to sort out the damp patch on the ceiling ages ago.'

'I'm hopeless in a crisis,' said Clarity mournfully.

'Well, my flowerpetal,' said Laurence, 'you know the solution – move in with me.'

Whether it was because her mother was tired, very wet, pre-menstrual, post-menstrual or just plain stupid, Tansy never worked out, but Clarity's next words hit her like a bombshell.

'I will,' she said, smiling with relief. '*We* will. I'll put the house on the market first thing tomorrow.'

THURSDAY

3.30 a.m.

The nightmare from hell

'Want to see the lions, Daddy. Now, Daddy. Now.'

'How could Cleo have done it? How could she?' Mum's voice shouting.

'Lettie – she could have been killed!'

'We won't tell the children what really happened ... what really happened ... what really happened ...'

Cleo woke up shaking from head to foot.

She knew what had really happened. She had let the handbrake off. She had made the car roll backwards. She, Cleo Greenway, had nearly killed her own sister.

And, because of that, no one had really loved her ever since.

6.45 a.m.

Being rudely awakened

'Holly, darling, wake up! We've got an early start!'

Angela Vine flung back her daughter's duvet and shook her shoulder.

'Mum!' Holly rolled over in disgust. 'It's the middle of the night.'

'Oh, don't be ridiculous, Holly, it's a quarter to seven, and I can't find the camping stove.'

I can't take insanity this early in the day, thought Holly.

'It's for the protest, you see,' her mother continued. 'Heating soup and stuff – only I can't find it and I remembered you had it when you went to Brownie camp.'

'Mum,' sighed Holly, 'I am fourteen years old. I was a Brownie when I was nine.'

'Yes, well, knowing your bedroom, it's probably still where you left it five years ago,' retorted her mother. 'Oh well, I'll just have to take a lot of thermos flasks, that's all. We can't have people dashing off all the time to buy coffees.'

'I thought,' said Holly, 'you were protesting in the hospital. They do have a cafeteria, you know.'

Her mother looked at her in astonishment.

'Oh no, darling,' she said. 'We're all taking over the roundabout outside the hospital. That way we get maximum exposure. Bound to make it into the papers.'

This cannot get any worse, thought Holly.

'Deannie's made the skeleton, I've got my blood vessels, and Dilys Pugh has painted a poster which says

"Toot if you support us".'

I was wrong, thought Holly. It just got worse.

7.30 a.m.

Calling his bluff

'Morning, Cleo!' Roy was standing at the hob, scrambling eggs in an uncharacteristically domestic manner. 'Mum's gone – the film crew called to say the thermals are right for ballooning!'

'Oh, right.' Cleo slumped at the table, too gutted to think up even the mildest sarcastic retort. 'No eggs for me, thanks.'

Roy eyed her closely.

'You look shattered,' he said. 'Bad night?'

'Yes – no – sort of,' said Cleo.

'I'm looking forward to your moment of stardom on Saturday,' he said chattily. 'How's it going?'

'OK,' she said.

'Now tell me, what exactly are you singing?'

'Roy, I know you're trying to be kind, but you don't have to. I know you're only coming because Mum can't face it.'

'Can't face what?' Portia burst into the kitchen before Roy had the chance to protest.

'Coming to the choir finals,' said Cleo. 'Everyone knows I'll make a hash of it.'

'No you won't,' said Portia, who was obviously into her once-a-year effort at being nice. 'Once you are up there on the stage ... say, they can't use the school hall, can they?'

Cleo shook her head.

'It's at Massingham Manor now,' she said. 'It's supposed to be really posh.'

Portia looked from Cleo to Roy and back again.

'Massingham Manor?'

Cleo nodded.

Not that it matters where it is, she thought angrily. None of my family can be bothered to come.

11.30 a.m.

On a chilly roundabout opposite Dunchester General Hospital. Protesting — and not just about closures

'It's going awfully well, don't you think?' Angela Vine asked Deannie Bennett as they jiggled their cardboard skeleton up and down at passing traffic. 'We're attracting a lot of attention.'

'Mmm.' Deannie Bennett murmured half-heartedly.

'Perhaps we should switch to the banner,' suggested Angela. A passing motorist tooted his horn.

'SOC it to them: Save Our Casualty,' she shouted excitedly.

Deannie suddenly dropped the skeleton to the ground and turned to face Angela.

'Look,' she said in a rush, 'this is awfully embarrassing, and I don't quite know how to begin, but I need to talk to you.'

'*Put the flesh on the NHS!*' Angela shrieked. 'What's that, Deannie?'

'It's about Holly,' began Deannie.

Angela stopped shrieking and eyed her neighbour anxiously.

'She's been talking to Amy,' said Deannie.

'Oh, that's nice!' enthused Angela. 'You said you wanted Amy to get to know more people.'

'Well, actually, it wasn't,' Deannie asserted. 'It wasn't nice at all. In fact, it was rather horrid.'

Angela threw her banner to the ground and slumped down on to the grass.

'I rather think,' she said, patting the ground beside her, 'that you had better tell me everything.'

1.00 p.m.

On song

'One final practice, choir, and then into the coach, and up, up and away!' boomed Miss Saffrey who had clad her chest in the most unfortunate pink angora bolero for the occasion. 'We have about an hour at Massingham for you to get used to the acoustics and then I want you to rest your voices until Saturday.'

She rustled her papers and coughed.

'In the unfortunate absence of Oliver Pritchard –' she clenched her teeth in fury – 'Cleo will sing both solo verses – the music has been transposed, dear.'

'OK,' said Cleo.

Jade and Tansy looked at one another. They had expected the usual round of 'Oh, Miss Saffrey, I can't', but Cleo was just looking dully at the sheet music and not saying a word.

Miss Saffrey played a chord and the choir sang. Cleo's solo came and went. The choir sang some more.

'Cleopatra,' called Miss Saffrey, as the rest of the choir headed off to pile into the coach. 'You are looking very pale, and your singing was not up to scratch. Please don't tell me you are coming down with something? Only this is our first big chance, and what with Oliver ...'

Cleo stared at Miss Saffrey. Suddenly she didn't see her hearty teacher, always telling people to strive onwards and upwards. She saw a nervous, worried young woman who desperately wanted to prove that her choir was something special. Olly had let her down; it was up to Cleo to make sure that she gave it her all.

'I'm fine, Miss Saffrey,' she smiled. 'Just saving my voice a bit.'

Saffers beamed and slapped her on the back.

'Triff,' she said and strode off to flutter her eyelashes at the coach driver.

1.40 p.m.

En route to Massingham Manor

'Hey, Holly, isn't that your mum?' Tansy peered out of the coach window.

Holly's eyes followed her gaze. Angela Vine, clad in an ancient pair of green cord trousers and an anorak that should never have been allowed to see the light of day, was standing in the middle of the roundabout, dripping blackcurrant juice from her plastic tubing and shouting, 'Don't drain the lifeblood from Dunchester General!'

'Ye gods!' sighed Holly. 'She should be locked up.'

'And look,' said Jade gleefully, 'there's TV East. I bet she's going to be on the news.'

Why, thought Holly, can't I have a mother who keeps her mouth shut?

2.00 p.m.

Embarrassing or what?

'Driver, what appears to be the problem?' Mr Grubb strode up to the front of the coach as the vehicle slowed to a snail's pace.

'There appears to be some sort of incident ahead, sir,' said the driver.

The coach edged slowly round a bend with high hawthorn hedges on either side. As the open fields came into view, a policeman with a broad grin on his face flagged it down. Suddenly a roar of laughter echoed from the front of the coach.

'What's going on?' Jade asked Cleo, standing up to peer through the front windscreen.

'Oh no, look – it's hilarious!' Holly spluttered, grabbing Tansy's arm.

'What – I can't see.' Cleo pushed her head between theirs. And wished she hadn't.

Caught in the overhanging branches of a large sycamore tree, and swaying gently three metres above the road, was a balloon. A balloon shaped like a giant pair of frilly knickers. And clambering from the basket on to a precariously balanced ladder, dressed only in a bright red bra and pair of briefs, with a chiffon scarf unsuccessfully shielding the naughty bits, was Cleo's mother.

'Say, Cleo, that's your mum!'

'Hey, what's Mrs Greenway doing in a tree?'

'Look, the cameras are rolling! It must be a film!'

I think, if it's all the same with you God, I'd like to die now, here, quite quietly, behind this seat. Because if I remain upright, I am going to kill my mother.

2.05 p.m.

Just go, Mum

'Is your mum really in a movie? You never said!' Tansy was clearly impressed.

'It's a TV ad,' said Cleo with a sigh, wishing that everyone would come away from the coach windows and stop observing her parent making a total idiot of herself. 'And would you brag about your mother running round the countryside half-naked?'

'At least she's glamorous,' sighed Holly. 'Unlike mine.'

There was a round of applause as Diana took the last step down from the ladder. She looked up at the coachload of peering West Greeners.

'Hi, kids!' she called out as a member of the film crew slipped a coat round her shoulders. 'Sorry for the little drama!'

The woman has no shame, thought Cleo, averting her eyes and praying that her mother would shut up.

'You are so lucky,' sighed Tansy, 'to have a mother with ambition.'

I think I would settle, thought Cleo, for one who had a grasp of normal behaviour.

2.20 p.m.

'Right, choir, we shall park the coach in this field and you just follow the path round behind the stable block and up the gravel drive to the house. We will assemble on the front steps in ten minutes.'

Everyone shoved and pushed to get off the bus.

'Well, Cleopatra, are we to see a second Greenway star in the firmament of show business on Saturday?' grinned Mr Grubb, who liked rubbing salt into wounds. 'Like mother, like daughter, eh?'

Cleo glared and said nothing. There was really nothing to say.

2.25 p.m.

My worst nightmare ...

'Wow! It's massive!' cried Tansy as they rounded the corner on to the gravel driveway.

'Look at that entrance!' said Jade. 'Grand or what?'

Cleo stood stock still and stared. Around her the voices of the clamouring choir members blurred into one echoing sound. She didn't move.

It was all there. Just like the dream. Every detail. The long gravel drive, the huge spreading cedar tree. And the lions. The four great stone lions, two either side of the steps leading to the front door.

'Daddy, I want to see the lions. Now, Daddy.'

Their car had been right there. On the left. Where the driveway sloped down to the wrought-iron gates.

Portia sitting astride a lion. 'I want a turn, me Daddy, now Daddy.'

Crunching gravel. 'I'm driving, Daddy! Look at me!'

Mummy running down the steps.

And a scream. A long, loud, never-ending scream.

Only this time, the scream was Cleo's.

2.26 p.m

... comes true

It seemed like a lifetime, but it was only a second. Everyone was looking at her. Her heart was pounding in her chest, and she felt as if her head was about to burst open.

This was the place. This was where she had done it. She might even be standing on the very patch of gravel where Lettie had lain so motionless and still.

'Cleo! Cleo!' Jade's voice seemed to be coming from a long way away.

Sirens wailing. Lettie gone. Mummy gone. Daddy too. Portia and Cleo in a car with a lady in a long funny dress.

'The little one did it, you know.'

'Cleo, are you OK?'

Cleo's stomach heaved and her head swam. And then the whole world went black.

2.40 p.m.

Feeling a fool

'Honestly, I'm fine now ... Yes, really ... No, of course I can sing ... Yes, I expect that was it – the coach. Yes, winding country lanes, of course. Sorry, Miss Saffrey.'

2.55 p.m.

Singing in a trance

'I can't go, Roy, I simply can't do it.'
    This is where it happened. That's why they won't come and watch me. This is where I did it.

3.30 p.m.

I just want to go home.

4.15 p.m.

Moment of truth

Holly let herself into her house and headed for the stairs.
    'Holly! I want a word with you!' Her mother was standing in the doorway of the kitchen with an extremely fierce expression on her face.

'If it's about my bedroom, I'll tidy it later,' she began.

'I wish that's all it was,' said her mother grimly. 'Sit down.'

Holly sat.

'Mrs Bennett has been talking to me about you,' she said.

Holly perked up.

'I gather you had words with Amy,' her mother began. 'And not very kind ones either, as I understand it.'

Holly stopped perking. The little toe-rag! She'd obviously gone bleating to Paul's mum in search of sympathy. Pathetic.

'You will go over to Mrs Bennett right now and listen to what she has to say,' ordered her mother. 'And I rather think you have a whole lot of apologizing to do.'

'Mum! Get real!' Holly protested. 'It's nothing to do with her.'

'Oh, isn't it?' said Angela. 'Go. Now.'

'But –'

'Or I stop your allowance for three months.'

Holly went.

4.25 p.m.

Moment of reckoning

'Ah, Holly, I've been expecting you. Come in.'

Mrs Bennett led Holly through to the kitchen.

'Holly, I think I had better come straight to the point,' began Deannie Bennett briskly. 'I gather you've been frightening Amy.'

'Frightening her?' Holly couldn't believe her ears. 'That's ridiculous! All I did was tell her to lay off Paul.'

The words had slipped out before she could stop them. A glance at Mrs Bennett's face told her that the last remark had not been a well chosen one.

'And I suppose you think you own Paul?' Mrs Bennett demanded. 'Well, before you started laying into poor Amy, why didn't you talk to Paul? Find out the facts?'

Holly had had enough of all this 'poor Amy' business.

'Because he kept ignoring me!' she retorted. 'I asked him to spend an evening with me, and he just went off with that Amy girl!'

'So you,' said Mrs Bennett, 'decided to put Amy straight?'

Holly nodded.

'Perhaps I was a bit over the top,' she admitted, trying to belatedly butter up Paul's mum, 'but I only told her what she needed to hear.'

Mrs Bennett sighed.

'That's the point,' she said. 'You were wasting your time.'

Holly frowned. It wasn't up to Paul's mum to tell her what to do.

'What do you mean?'

At that moment the kitchen door opened and Amy burst in.

Amy stopped dead at the sight of Holly.

Holly gasped.

Amy's thick, long hair was pulled back off her face. She was wearing hearing aids in both ears.

'Amy is my niece,' said Mrs Bennett, 'and she is profoundly deaf.'

4.35 p.m.

Feeling awful

'I'm so sorry, really I am,' Holly said for the fifth time.

Amy nodded.

'Thank you,' she said, carefully enunciating each word.

'You see,' said Mrs Bennett, 'if you talk slowly she can lip-read really well, but when you yelled at her, she just got scared. We were all out, she had forgotten her key and she didn't know what was going on.'

Amy started signing quickly to her aunt.

'Amy says she can hear a bit with the help of her hearing aid – but only when there are no other noises. There was so much traffic that nothing you said made sense.'

'I thought,' admitted Holly, 'that she was a mate of Paul's – she got off the Bishop Agnew bus with him and –'

Mrs Bennett interrupted. 'Amy is staying with us while her mum is in hospital, aren't you, dear?' she said. 'We thought it would be good for her to spend some time at Paul's school because she hopes to go into mainstream education next year.'

Holly bit her lip. Paul wasn't in love with Amy – he had obviously been gazing at her so intently simply so that she could read his lips.

'I've been an idiot,' she admitted. 'Will you tell her that? Will she forgive me?'

Amy stared at her lips, then turned and flounced out of the room.

'Not,' said Mrs Bennett, 'if you treat her as if she

wasn't even here. She's deaf, not stupid. I think perhaps now you had better go.'

6.30 p.m.

At home. In a daze

The whole afternoon had passed in a blur. Recalling it now was like watching snatches of a film trailer. Miss Saffrey patting her hand and giving her a glass of water. Cleo hearing her own voice reassuring Miss Saffrey that, honestly, she was fine and it was just the time of the month or maybe the motion of the coach and there was no need to phone parents or anything like that.

Standing in the choir singing while her head was filled with pictures of ambulances and stone lions and cedar trees. Sitting in the coach chatting and not really hearing the words she was speaking. Walking home, watching TV, doing homework, all of it seeming as though it were happening to someone else.

And now she was sitting at the supper table trying to force food into her mouth while the rest of the family behaved as if today had been a perfectly ordinary day.

'... and I had to climb down this ladder in front of all these West Green children!' Diana chortled merrily. 'It was hilarious, wasn't it, Cleo?'

'... and I told Russell that unless he got his act together once and for all, that was it!' Portia was declaring.

'... so can I go to France, Mum? Please say I can go – there's this form you have to fill in ...' Lettie was waving paper in her mother's face.

'... more expense, I suppose?' Roy demanded.

Cleo looked at their faces. She wanted to stand up, right there and then, and demand to be told everything. The whole truth. All of it.

Except she knew the truth. And it was awful.

'I don't feel very well,' she said. 'I'm going to bed.'

7.30 p.m.

Eyes firmly closed

'Cleo, are you OK?'

Lie still and pretend to be asleep.

'She's asleep, Mum!' Portia yelled downstairs.

If I had been asleep, I certainly wouldn't be now, thought Cleo.

9.00 p.m.

Wanting to curl up and die

Holly stared blindly at her French homework. How could she have messed up like that? Far from getting Paul back she had probably lost him for ever. And his mum thought she was the lowest of the low. And life was as good as over.

'Holly, can I come in? I've brought you a mug of tea.'

Angela Vine took one look at her daughter's face, put the tea on the dressing table and gave her a hug.

'It's not the end of the world,' she said. 'You've

apologized and you've learned a lesson – now let's forget it.'

'I can't,' sobbed Holly. 'What if Paul never speaks to me again?'

'If he doesn't,' said her mother stoically, 'he was never worth having in the first place. I'm sure that when his mother tells him the whole story, he will respect you for admitting you were in the wrong.'

'You do?' Her mother could be quite sensible at times, Holly thought.

'And besides,' added Angela, 'you're far too young to be filling your head with boys.'

Then again, the sensible times never lasted very long.

7.30 a.m.

Faking it

She had worked it all out. She knew what she had to do and she knew she had to do it today. Which meant getting out of going to school.

She pushed open the kitchen door, her hand clamped to her forehead.

'Morning, darling! How are you feeling?' Diana was standing at the kitchen sink dressed in a bright-red caftan and embroidered slippers looking as if was about to attend a gala première rather than do the washing up.

'Awful,' said Cleo, which was at least halfway true. 'I don't think I can make it to school.'

Diana frowned.

'Oh, what a nuisance!' she said. 'I've got such a busy day – we're putting the advert in the bag, and then there's –'

'It's OK,' said Cleo hurriedly. 'You go – I'll be fine. I'll just sleep.'

8.00 a.m.

Shock horror

'Mum, there's a man in the front garden!'

Tansy peered through the window. A short guy was hammering a 'For Sale' board into the lawn.

Tansy's heart sank. She was going through with it. Time was running out.

'They say we should get one hundred and forty thousand for it,' said Clarity, eyeing her daughter nervously. 'And the agent has already got someone who wants to look over it. That's good, isn't it?'

'It's disastrous,' said Tansy.

8.55 a.m.

At the school gates

'Can you believe my mother could do that!' exclaimed Tansy as she and Holly turned into the school yard. 'She must be world's biggest idiot.'

Holly shook her head.

'I guess I have that title,' she said miserably. 'I've really messed up this time. Amy is Paul's cousin. And she's deaf. And I think I've blown it big time.'

'Tell me,' said Tansy.

Holly told her.

'And I don't know what to do to show Paul that I'm sorry, and that I'm not really a horrid person,' she said. 'I

101

waved this morning as he left for school and he ignored me. Just turned the other way.'

Tansy thought.

'I've got this book,' she said. 'That should do it.'

'What book? What are you on about?'

'Trust me,' said Tansy. 'I have a plan.'

9.30 a.m.

On the telephone

'Hi, Dad, it's Cleo.'

'Cleo! Not at school?' Max sounded anxious.

'No – listen, Dad, I need to see you. Now. Today.'

There was a pause.

'Is something wrong? Sweetheart, I can't just drop everything, I'm at the office and –'

'OK, so if you won't come to me, I'll get a train and come to you.' Cleo sounded a lot braver than she felt. 'It's really important to me, Dad. It's about Lettie's accident.'

This time the silence was even longer.

'I'm fed up with secrets, Dad!' Cleo felt a sob catch in her throat. 'No one will tell me anything and yesterday I was there, at Massingham Manor, for the rehearsals, and I remembered the tree and the stone lions and being in the car and ...'

Her voice trailed away.

'Where's your mother? Isn't she there with you? Can't you ask her?'

Cleo's sobs died as her anger rose.

'She's at work, and no, Dad, I can't ask her, because

like you, she fobs me off with half-truths.

I am fourteen years old, Dad. I have a right to know.'

Another silence.

'Is that why you left us? Because of what I did?'

'YOU? Darling, no.' Her father's voice was faint and husky. 'I'm coming over. I'll be with you in an hour.'

11.00 a.m.

Wondering how to begin

Cleo sat opposite her dad, watching him nervously sipping a cup of coffee and thinking how much she missed having him around.

'Dad, you have to tell me everything. Lettie's getting teased about her scars, and I can't talk to her properly because I don't think she knows I did it and –'

'You didn't do anything, Cleo. I did.' Max stared into the mug of coffee he was gripping in both hands.

'But in my dream, Mum keeps saying, "How could Cleo do a thing like that?" '

Max nodded.

'You're right, she did say that. Repeatedly, for weeks after the accident.'

Cleo's heart lurched.

'So she does blame me?'

Her father shook his head.

'No, no, darling, don't you see?' he stressed. 'Listen – she was saying "*How could* Cleo *do a thing like that?*" She knew that a tiny five-year-old wouldn't have had the strength to let a handbrake off a big car like that. She knew that wasn't how it happened.'

Cleo paused, hardly daring to breathe.

'She knew it was me,' said her father, with a catch in his voice. 'Only I was too much of a coward to face up to what I had done. You were alone in the car – it seems I found it easier to blame you.'

Cleo swallowed.

Her father took a deep breath.

'Mum had been filming at Massingham Manor for a TV series, some costume drama about the Civil War ...'

The ladies in long dresses ...

'... and I had taken you three to fetch her. I took Lettie out of her car seat and Portia ran off to play on those big lions ...'

Four stone lions. Portia riding the smiling one.

'... and then you started screaming and banging on the car window because you wanted to go too. Only you had German measles – or was it chickenpox? – and were infectious and so I said you had to stay where you were.'

So that bit was true. Mum wasn't lying then.

'Then Portia started fooling around and I thought she would fall, and I leaped out of the car and slammed the door, and as it slammed, the wheels began to move and I turned and there was Lettie, toddling off behind and ...'

Her father's voice broke and he put his head in his hands.

'I pulled on the handbrake, but it was too late. Lettie's leg was under the car.'

He lifted his face and looked at Cleo.

'It was nothing to do with you, darling. It was all my fault.'

11.45 a.m.

Two pots of tea and a dozen soggy tissues later

'Cleo! I'm back, angel. How are you?'

The front door slammed as Diana's voice echoed down the hallway.

'I thought I would pop back to see if you were feeling – oh!' She caught sight of Cleo's dad and the smile faded from her lips. 'What are you doing here?'

Max Greenway held up a hand.

'I haven't come to cause trouble,' he said hastily. 'I've come to make amends.'

'I asked him to come, Mum,' interrupted Cleo. 'I'm fed up with nightmares and half-truths, and I decided that I had to find out what really happened.'

'Oh.' Diana's face seemed to age in a moment, and she sank into the nearest armchair and began twisting her fingers in her lap. 'And what has your father told you?'

'The truth,' said Max. 'And not before time.'

Noon.

Letting it all out

'But I still don't understand why you let me think, all those years, that it was my fault!' shouted Cleo, who had grown more angry the more she had thought about it. 'How could you pretend it was my fault?'

'We didn't,' said her mother. 'Your father ...'

'We didn't,' said her father at the same instant. 'Your mother ...'

They stopped.

'For weeks, I tried to convince myself and everyone else that you, Cleo, must have let off the handbrake,' said her father miserably.

'And I knew full well that you wouldn't have had the strength,' added her mother.

'I knew no one would punish a five-year-old child,' continued her father, 'and somehow I blanked out the fact that it was my responsibility and just let everyone go on believing the lie.'

'And I was too worried about Lettie and her operations and whether she would walk again, to argue,' sighed her mother.

'In the end,' said her father, 'I had to face up to the fact that it was my fault. I told your mother. She was the one who decided that we would never let you kids know what really happened.'

There was a long silence. In the corner, the old carriage clock ticked. Somewhere in the distance a dog barked and a car door slammed.

'So you let me go on blaming myself all this time?' Cleo choked out the words as her eyes filled with tears.

'No!' Both parents replied simultaneously.

'It wasn't meant to be like that,' said Diana, pulling a tissue from the box on the coffee table and wiping her eyes. 'I was so afraid that if Lettie grew up knowing it was Max's fault, it would ruin their relationship – ruin his relationship with all of you, in fact. I thought you were too little to remember what had happened, and, of course, that was crazy of me. And I bribed Portia to keep quiet, made her promise never to speak of it again. It was so wrong of me, I can see that now.'

She turned to face Cleo, her eyes brimming with tears.

'Can you ever forgive me?'

Cleo opened her mouth to speak, but her father got there first.

'You mustn't blame Mum, Cleo,' he said firmly. 'Blame me, hate me, but not her. She only did what she thought was for the best.'

Cleo nodded.

'I know,' she said. 'But, Dad, I thought you left because you couldn't bear to be near me – so if I didn't do it, why did you go?'

Max sighed.

'Sometimes people just don't get on, Cleo. Mum and I tried, we really did. But she blamed me for the accident, and then I blamed her for spending so much time with Lettie that there was never time for us, and we argued and shouted and then –'

'And then he met Fleur and walked out!'

'No, it wasn't like that – you were always the one –'

'STOP IT!' Cleo shouted. 'I don't need this. None of us need this. I'm glad you've told me the truth, and I'm glad it wasn't my fault. I love you both – we all do. So please, don't fight. Can't you just be friends?'

Neither of her parents said a word.

Cleo took a deep breath.

'I want you both to come to the finals tomorrow,' she said.

'I can't!' Diana gasped. 'The memories ...'

'No way, darling, it's not on,' protested her father. 'It will bring it all back ...'

'I see,' said Cleo, trying to keep her voice calm. 'So what

happened in the past matters more to you than what's happening to your kids now, does it? Don't you think I just want you to be there for me now?'

Diana and Max exchanged glances.

'I'll come,' said Max quietly.

'Me too,' said Diana. 'Provided that woman ...' She stopped. 'Bring Fleur too, why don't you?' she said tightly. 'It might make things easier for you.'

Cleo ran to her mother and hugged her.

'I love you,' she said. 'Both of you. So much.'

It was as she was on her way to the kitchen to make yet another pot of tea that she heard her parents talking softly.

'She's changed,' she heard her father say. 'She used to be such a little mouse.'

'She gets her spunkiness from me, of course,' said her mother.

Cleo smiled. It didn't matter to her where it came from. She was just glad it had arrived.

1.00 p.m.

Enough is enough

'I'm going to school now,' Cleo told her parents. 'I've got things to get sorted.'

'Oh, darling, surely it's not worth going in now?' Diana protested.

'Oh yes it is,' said Cleo. 'If I have anything to do with it, it will be very well worth it indeed.'

1.35 p.m.

Settling a score

'Olly! Hang on!' Cleo panted up to him as he headed for the stairs.

'I thought you were ill,' said Olly, turning to face her. 'Jade told me about you fainting.'

He eyed her as if she might break into pieces in front of his eyes.

'Old Saffers was doing her nut thinking you wouldn't sing. With me not doing it, she –'

'But you will be doing it,' said Cleo firmly. 'We both will.'

Olly shook his head vehemently.

'Not me,' he said. 'I have my reasons.'

'Oh really,' said Cleo. 'Well, let me tell you my reasons for never, ever wanting to go back to that place.'

She told him.

'... So if I can do it, you can.'

Olly looked at her for a long time.

'But when you sing, everyone thinks it's special,' said Olly softly. 'When I sing, my mates titter.'

Cleo frowned.

'But you're the star alto – you've won prizes, you –'

'That's the whole point!' exploded Olly. 'I'm fourteen. And my voice hasn't broken. You wouldn't understand, you're a girl, but I feel such a kid, so weedy ...'

Suddenly Cleo understood.

'I guess that when you want something to happen a whole lot, it seems like it never will,' she said thoughtfully.

'But don't you see – once your voice does break, you won't be able to sing like you do now. Don't you want to make the most of it while you still can?'

He didn't look convinced.

'As for weedy – all my friends think you're a total dish,' she said with a grin. 'You can't deprive them of a quick swoon while you sing.'

Olly smiled weakly.

'Really?'

'Really,' said Cleo firmly. 'Don't you fancy being the school pin-up?'

Olly grinned.

'Maybe I can hack it after all,' he said.

Cleo nodded.

'And Cleo?'

'Yes?'

'Thanks.'

4.45 p.m.

Mark, learn and inwardly digest

'There you are!' Tansy handed Holly a battered book. 'Get that sussed and you'll be home and dry.'

Holly peered at the page and her face lightened.

'That's brilliant!' she said, hugging Tansy. 'Thanks so much – only it's going to take ages to learn this and –'

'Defeatist!' Tansy admonished. 'Just do it.'

10.45 p.m.

In bed

It was hard, thought Holly, much harder than it looked. She had only learned a bit of the book, not nearly enough for Tansy's plan to work.

She had to keep awake. She had to do some more.

Her future happiness depended on it.

If only her eyes wouldn't keep closing.

SATURDAY

9.30 a.m.

A word of praise

'Holly, you'll be late. Take your nose out of that book and get moving.'

Holly went on reading.

'What is this anyway?' demanded her mother, snatching the book from her hands. 'Some horror nonsense, or that awful – Oh. Oh, I see. Gracious. Well done, you.'

Holly looked up. Her mother smiled.

'Taking positive action, I see,' said Angela. 'You're getting more like me every day.'

Heaven forbid, thought Holly, and went to brush her teeth.

10.30 a.m.

Anxious

'Are you OK?' Jade touched Cleo's arm as they all walked

towards the doorway of Massingham Manor.

Cleo nodded and looked anxiously over her shoulder to the field where the visitors' cars were parked.

'I can't see my mum's car yet,' she said. 'I hope she'll turn up.'

'Of course she will,' said Jade. 'Why wouldn't she?'

'No reason,' said Cleo.

10.45 a.m.

'Now, choir,' said Miss Saffrey, who for reasons best known to herself was dressed in a bright-pink taffeta skirt of indeterminate age, 'we are on third. I want you to give it your all – sing as though you were never going to sing again.'

'Which I'm not,' muttered Oliver to Cleo.

'Hush!' Miss Saffrey admonished him. 'Cleo, stop staring round the audience in that manner. It's most intrusive.'

They're not here. Neither of them. They're not coming after all. They promised.

She followed disconsolately as the rest of the choir filed into their reserved seats at the side of the ornate banqueting room.

'This place is amazing!' breathed Tansy, staring up at the painted ceiling.

'There's your mum!' Jade nudged Tansy. 'Who's she talking to?'

Tansy peered across the heads of the audience. And grinned.

'That's Jonathan Pitt-Warren,' she said proudly, noting

with satisfaction that Jonathan's hand was resting lightly on her mum's arm. 'He owns this place. My mum's doing some work ... he and my mother are really close.'

Jade's amazed expression was reward enough. For now.

11.40 a.m.

Relief

'We're on!' Miss Saffrey's neck had turned red with agitation and her chest had taken on a life all of its own and was heaving dramatically.

They haven't come, thought Cleo. Her stomach felt like lead and the last thing she wanted to do was sing.

The music started. The choir began the first verse. Cleo choked back a sob and tried to lose herself in the music.

'*Steal away, steal away steal away, oooh, steal away ...*'
The music rose to a crescendo.

'*Steal away home, I ain't got long to stay here ...*'
Miss Saffrey made lifting gestures with her hands, encouraging the choir to look up and sing to the rafters.

Cleo raised her eyes. And almost missed a note. There, leaning over the minstrels' gallery looking straight at her, were her family: Mum, Dad, Fleur, Roy, Portia, even Lettie.

Cleo beamed. They had come. Despite everything, they were here.

She had made it happen. For the first time ever, she had stood firm and got results. And now she knew she could do anything.

The chorus faded. Miss Saffrey turned to face her. She

lifted her baton and counted her in.

Cleo began to sing.

11.55 a.m.

'You were brilliant!' Olly gave her a friendly punch on the shoulder. 'Ace!'

'So were you!' said Cleo. 'Although that last line ...'

'I know, isn't it cool?' said Olly. 'I think it's happening at last.'

'What's happening?' Trig pushed through the huddles of singers to reach them.

'Nothing,' said Cleo, and was deeply satisfied to see the worried look on Trig's face.

1.00 p.m.

Family feeling

All the choirs had finished singing and everyone was filing into the dining room for drinks and nibbles while the judges made their final decision.

Cleo spotted her family striding purposefully in the opposite direction towards the front door.

'Mum! Dad!' She pushed through the throng to reach them.

'Oh, Cleo! Darling! You were splendid, quite splendid!' Her mum gave her a hug.

'I was so proud!' Her dad squeezed her arm.

'Really?'

'Believe me, he was,' said Fleur, who had hung back from the others. 'He kept saying "that's my girl" – I almost had to gag him!'

Cleo grinned.

'I just hope these babies –' she patted her tummy – 'will be half as clever.'

Cleo shot an anxious glance towards her mother.

Diana took a deep breath.

'I forgot,' she said. 'Congratulations. I'm very happy for both of you.'

1.30 p.m.

The shattering of a dream

'Have another sausage,' Clarity urged Tansy. 'That way you won't need so much supper.'

'Now there's a thought!' boomed a deep voice. To Tansy's horror, Jonathan Pitt-Warren had appeared at her mother's left shoulder. 'I'm glad the food is to your liking.'

'Scrummy,' said Clarity without a shadow of shame.

'Your house is amazing, Mr Pitt-Warren,' said Tansy hastily, in the hope of showing him that at least one member of the family knew how to behave. 'It must be great to live here.'

Jonathan laughed.

'Too big, too draughty, and far too expensive,' he said.

'So why did you buy it?' asked Clarity. Tansy cringed.

'Oh, we're not going to live here permanently,' he said. We? thought Tansy with a jolt.

'My wife would hate to be out of London for very long,'

he said.

Wife? What do you mean, wife? thought Tansy.

'We bought it as an investment – we plan to turn it into timeshare apartments with a health club, sports facilities, that sort of thing. And, of course,' he added with a grin, 'the most magnificent gardens in Dunchestershire.'

Clarity laughed.

'I am counting on your mother,' he said, turning to Tansy.

So was I, thought Tansy. And look where it got me!

2.00 p.m.

Moment of glory

'And so, after much deliberation, the judges have awarded the title of Choir of the Year to ...'

Cleo held her breath. Tansy chewed her thumb. Jade closed her eyes.

'... Buckingham House School!'

There was a burst of applause. Miss Saffrey fixed a smile to her lips and tried to clap enthusiastically. Cleo worked hard at not bursting into tears.

'And now for the individual prize,' said the judge.

Cleo frowned. No one had said anything about any more prizes.

'All the soloists were excellent,' said the judge. 'But one stood out in a class of her own. The award for Soloist of the Year goes to Cleopatra Greenway.'

The whole of West Green's contingent burst into an uproar.

'Good on you, Cleo! Well done!'

Cleo sat open-mouthed. She had won a prize. She never won prizes. She was the best soloist. She had never been best at anything.

'And now to present the prizes, we are delighted to welcome Jonathan Pitt-Warren, the owner of Massingham Manor and director of PW Leisure.'

Cleo's heart pounded as she walked up the steps on to the stage, and received a silver cup and an envelope.

'This way, love!' Cameras flashed. People stamped and clapped. Cleo looked up into the gallery. Her mum and dad were hugging each other.

And that was the best reward of all.

2.30 p.m.

Added bonus

'Say, Cleo, that was brilliant!' Trig beamed at her. 'How about we go out tonight to celebrate?'

Cleo's heart leapt.

'Go out?'

Trig nodded.

'I've got some spare cash – we could get a pizza and go to a movie, or go bowling or –'

'You really want to?' Cleo asked.

Trig frowned.

'Sure, I want to,' he said. 'It's been ages.'

'I thought ...' Cleo began. And stopped.

'Thought what?' asked Trig.

'Nothing,' said Cleo.

It wouldn't do to let him know she had been bothered. It wouldn't do at all.

3.30 p.m.

'Bye, Dad. Bye, Fleur – thanks for coming!'

Cleo and her sisters piled into the back of Roy's car, Cleo clutching her trophy in one hand.

Roy started the engine. It spluttered and stopped.

'Just go, Roy, now, please,' her mum said through clenched teeth.

The engine fired. The car moved. Down the drive and out through the gates. Diana sighed audibly and her shoulders dropped.

'Mum,' said Cleo.

'Yes, darling?'

'Thanks,' said Cleo.

'What for?'

'For being so brave.'

3.40 p.m.

'I'm scared.' Holly and Tansy were squashed into Clarity's van, enduring a boneshaking journey home. 'What if I forget it all? What if it doesn't work?'

'It'll work,' said Tansy confidently. 'But make sure Paul's there before you start, OK?'

'Start what?' asked Clarity, crunching the gears. 'What are you two plotting now?'

'Mum, just drive, OK?' said Tansy.

119

5.30 p.m.

Making amends

Holly rang the front door of Paul's house, feeling incredibly sick. She heard footsteps. The door opened.

It was Paul.

'Hi!' It came out as a strangled squeak.

'Hello,' said Paul. And stood there.

'Look,' said Holly. 'Can I come in? I need to speak to Amy.'

'Why?'

'It won't take a minute and then I'll go,' said Holly in desperation. 'Please.'

Paul stepped to one side.

'OK. Come in – she's in the kitchen.'

Holly took a deep breath. She pushed back her sleeves and bit her lip.

'Hi, Amy.' That took ages. This sign language was hard enough with the book, but doing it from memory was even harder.

She was aware of Paul's eyes watching her. Amy began to smile.

'Would you like to ...?' Holly stopped. She couldn't remember the next bit.

'Would I like what?' urged Amy carefully and slowly.

Holly pointed to her house and then signed again.

'To ... to listen to tapes ...' And clamped her hand to her mouth. That was wrong. She couldn't listen. She couldn't hear.

'Sorry,' she said out loud. 'I meant ...'

Amy grinned.

'To talk?'

Holly nodded.

'That would be great,' said Amy. 'Can I come now?'

Holly suddenly felt nervous. It was difficult to know how loud to talk. Or what to do next.

'It's OK,' giggled Amy, 'I don't bite. Let's go.'

'Don't be long,' said Paul firmly. He grinned at Holly. 'Because I'm taking Holly out later on.'

'You are?' Holly hardly dared to breathe.

'I am,' said Paul, 'if you'll let me.'

6.15 p.m.

Rejoicing

'Tansy? It's me, Holly. I did it. And it's OK. Amy came over and we talked ... Yes, she's got this machine thing which I speak into and she can hear at least some of it. And guess what? I'm going out ... With Paul ... In half an hour. What do you mean, where? Who cares where? I'll sit on the town dump if it means being with him. Oh and Tansy? Thanks. You're a mate.'

6.30 p.m.

Sisterly confidences

'Can I come in?'

Portia hovered in the doorway of Cleo's bedroom.

'Yes, sure.' The shock of hearing her sister actually ask permission to do anything almost robbed Cleo of the power of speech.

'Dad said you talked,' said Portia in clipped tones. 'About the accident. I guess you know it wasn't your fault.'

Cleo nodded. 'It's a relief, I can tell you,' she said. 'Maybe now the dreams will go.'

'So what did he say about me?'

'About you?'

'Don't pretend!' retorted Portia. 'He got out of the car because I was being naughty and that's why he forgot to put on the brake and that's why he put Lettie down and ...'

Cleo looked at her sister's tense face and thought fast.

'If I hadn't been naughty ...'

'Hang on,' interrupted Cleo. 'He told me he got out of the car because ... Her brain raced ahead. 'Because Lettie wanted a wee. He didn't mention you being naughty.'

'He didn't?'

Cleo shook her head.

Portia's face relaxed.

'I thought Dad ... oh, never mind. By the way,' she said, 'why are you all glammed up?'

'I'm going out with Trig,' she said.

'Oh,' said Portia, 'is that all?'

It's enough, thought Cleo. For now, it's quite enough.

'You look cool,' added Portia. 'Really sassy.'

Soloist of the Year and sassy with it, thought Cleo. Not bad for one day.

SUNDAY

9.45 a.m.

Negotiating a sale

'And this is my daughter's bedroom.'

Tansy glowered at the fresh-faced couple who were holding hands and oohing and aahing at every room in the cottage.

'It's lovely,' said the woman.

'There's a damp patch on the ceiling, and it gets very cold,' insisted Tansy. 'And the window rattles in the wind.'

Clarity glared at her.

'We love it, don't we, Josh?' said the woman.

The man nodded.

'It's so full of atmosphere,' he said.

'That,' said Tansy, 'will be the ghost.'

The woman paled.

'Ghost?' she said.

'What utter nonsense!' retorted Clarity. 'She doesn't want to move and she's trying to put you off.'

'You did say, Mum,' said Tansy with wide eyes, 'that I always had to tell the truth. Have I done wrong?'

'I think we'll leave it for now,' said the guy, hastily. 'Thanks all the same.'

Yes! thought Tansy, silently punching the air. There were times when a vivid imagination came in awfully handy.

10.30 a.m.

Maternal recriminations

Clarity rammed the car into gear and pumped the accelerator in a needlessly violent manner.

'How could you do that, Tansy?' she stormed, spinning the wheel and turning into Weston Way. 'How could you be so stupid?'

'You're a fine one to talk!' shouted Tansy. 'Selling our house to move in with a chinless wonder is hardly the height of common sense!'

'Well, let me tell you this, young lady,' said Clarity. 'This is my life and I will do with it as I please. Now we are going round to Laurence's so that you can see your new bedroom and I expect you to be civil, do you understand?'

Tansy turned and looked out of the van window. She wasn't going to give her mother the satisfaction of seeing her cry.

11.00 a.m.

In the house from hell

'And I thought Tansy could have this room!' Laurence threw

open the door. Lurid green-and-yellow wallpaper hit Tansy between the eyeballs and the smell of mothballs wrinkled her nose.

'Lovely,' said Clarity. 'Isn't it, Tansy?'

'It's foul,' said Tansy turning her back and walking out of the room. 'It smells.'

'Oh, Tansy,' said Clarity lightly. 'It'll be fine – you can burn some of those nice ylang-ylang incense sticks of mine and –'

'Oh no,' said Laurence. 'Not in my house. Those things play havoc with my sinuses.'

He paused.

'In fact, maybe we should talk house rules for a minute,' he said. 'I know you two have been living, well, somewhat casually of late, and I do realize that it was all down to lack of money, but I take a pride in my home.'

Oh terrific, thought Tansy.

'There's a shed in the garden for you to potter, flowerpetal, so none of your planting out on the kitchen table, please. Oh, and I don't like this habit of trays in front of the television – it's so bad for the digestion.'

Tansy raised her eyebrows.

'Is breathing allowed?' she asked. 'Or does that use up too much of your precious oxygen?'

Laurence's face clouded.

'Clarity, are you going to allow her to speak to me like that?'

Tansy waited for the outburst.

'Yes, actually,' said Clarity, 'I rather think I am.'

11.55 a.m.

A lucky escape

'Pompous idiot!' Clarity slammed the van door shut and revved the engine. 'I can't live like that!'

Thank you, God. Thank you very, very much.

'How dare he tell me where to sit and how to eat? I may not be the model homemaker ...'

This is true, thought Tansy.

' ... but one does have to have a bit of fun.'

'So we're not moving?' ventured Tansy.

Clarity sighed.

'I guess not,' she said. 'Although how we are going to manage, I don't know. It will be OK while this work with Jonathan holds out, but once it's finished ...'

'Live for the moment, Mum,' advised Tansy wisely. 'Anything could turn up between now and then. Just be glad that you've escaped a lifetime with that wallpaper.'

Clarity turned to Tansy and burst out laughing.

'Oh, Tansy,' she said, 'I do love you.'

'I love you too,' said Tansy. 'Ever such a lot.'

2.30 p.m.

Hot line from Holly

'Does the phone ever stop ringing in this house?' complained Roy, in between shouting rude words at the England cricket team on Channel Four.

Cleo grabbed the phone.

'Cleo? It's Holly. I'm bored.'

'Are you?'

'Tansy's gone out because Andy's back, Jade's having tea with Scott's family, and I thought maybe you'd like to come round and we could have a good goss. What do you say?'

'Sorry, can't,' said Cleo smugly. 'Me and Trig are going skateboarding.'

'Skateboarding? You?'

'That's right.'

It was not often, thought Cleo with deep satisfaction, that her friend was rendered totally speechless.

4.00 p.m.

Trig threw his skateboard to one side and turned to Cleo.

'Can I ask you an enormous favour?'

Cleo nodded.

'Of course – what is it?'

'You have to promise not to laugh,' insisted Trig. 'And not to tell another living soul.'

Cleo frowned.

'I promise,' she said. 'Tell me.'

Trig pulled several sheets of paper from his jacket pocket and thrust them under her nose.

Time Travelling with Trig Roscoe

Think your home town is dull and boring?

Wish you lived somewhere else?

Once you've been on a Trig Roscoe Time Travel Trampabout, you'll see Dunchester through new eyes!

Cleo burst out laughing.

'I knew you'd think it was stupid!' Trig snatched the paper out of her hands. 'Forget I ever –'

'Hang on!' Cleo protested. 'I was laughing at that brilliant name – Time Travel Trampabout – it's great!'

'It is?'

'Brill – what's it all about?'

'There's this competition to win a whole month next summer working with a team of historians on an archeological dig, or a restoration project or anything you like,' he said, his whole face lighting up with excitement. 'You have to come up with a really cool idea for getting people who think history is mega-dull to take an interest, get involved. This is my idea.'

Cleo's eyes scanned the page. There were routes past haunted pubs, a walk round Dunchester castle ruins, even a Death Row Doddle past the old prison to the site of the old gallows.

'Were there really gallows in Dunchester?' gasped Cleo. 'I never knew.'

Trig beamed.

'See? It's taken me ages to research everything.'

'So that's what you've been so taken up with!' exclaimed Cleo. 'And I thought ...' She stopped.

'Thought what?'

'Nothing.'

Trig took the paper out of her hand.

'So you think it's a neat idea?'

'It's great – but what about this favour you wanted?'

'Will you walk the routes with me and tell me what you think of my instructions? I need the views of someone who's hopeless at History.'

'Oh cheers,' said Cleo. But she was grinning from ear to ear. She hadn't lost Trig to another girl. In fact, she hadn't lost him at all. Far from feeling hopeless, she couldn't remember when she had felt so good.

5.00 p.m.

Manic mother strikes again

'That was brilliant!' Cleo was red faced, breathless and bruised but exceedingly happy. 'Come in and have a drink.'

She opened the door and ushered Trig through. And stopped dead. Standing in the hallway was her mother.

Holding a mop in one hand and a small melon in the other and singing at the top of her voice.

'Darling? And Trig – long time no see!' She noted their puzzled stares. 'Orb and sceptre, darlings.'

She gestured to the mop and melon.

'I'm getting into the mood,' she enthused. 'I've just had a phone call asking me to play the Fairy Queen in the rep's production of *Iolanthe*. Aren't you pleased for me?'

'Is this in a theatre? Behind closed doors?' demanded Cleo.

Diana frowned and nodded.

'And does this character keep her clothes on throughout the whole production?'

'Well, of course she does, darling,' said her mother.

'Go for it,' said Cleo.

Sunday

Look out for more great

Book One

Book Two

Book Three

titles in the series:

Book Four

Book Five

Book Six

www.puffin.co.uk.www.puffin.co.uk.www.puffin.co.uk
bookinfo.competitions.news.games.sneakpreviews
www.puffin.co.uk.www.puffin.co.uk.www.puffin.co.uk
adventure.bestsellers.fun.coollinks.freestuff
www.puffin.co.uk.www.puffin.co.uk.www.puffin.co.uk
explore.yourshout.awards.toptips.authorinfo
www.puffin.co.uk.www.puffin.co.uk.www.puffin.co.uk
greatbooks.greatbooks.greatbooks.greatbooks
www.puffin.co.uk.www.puffin.co.uk.www.puffin.co.uk
reviews.poems.jokes.authorevents.audioclips
www.puffin.co.uk.www.puffin.co.uk.www.puffin.co.uk
interviews.e-mailupdates.bookinfo.competitions.news

www.puffin.co.uk

games.sneakpreviews.adventure.bestsellers.fun
www.puffin.co.uk.www.puffin.co.uk.www.puffin.co.uk
bookinfo.competitions.news.games.sneakpreviews
www.puffin.co.uk.www.puffin.co.uk.www.puffin.co.uk
adventure.bestsellers.fun.coollinks.freestuff
www.puffin.co.uk.www.puffin.co.uk.www.puffin.co.uk
explore.yourshout.awards.toptips.authorinfo
www.puffin.co.uk.www.puffin.co.uk.www.puffin.co.uk
greatbooks.greatbooks.greatbooks.greatbooks
www.puffin.co.uk.www.puffin.co.uk.www.puffin.co.uk
reviews.poems.jokes.authorevents.audioclips
www.puffin.co.uk.www.puffin.co.uk.www.puffin.co.uk

www.puffin.co.uk.www.puffin.co.uk.www.puffin.co.uk
ookinfo.competitions.news.games.sneakpreviews
www.puffin.co.uk.www.puffin.co.uk.www.puffin.co.uk
dventure.bestsellers.fun.coollinks.freestuff
www.puffin.co.uk.www.puffin.co.uk.www.puffin.co.uk
xplore.yourshout.awards.toptips.authorinfo
www.puffin.co.uk.www.puffin.co.uk.www.puffin.co.uk
reatbooks.greatbooks.greatbooks.greatbooks
www.puffin.co.uk.www.puffin.co.uk.www.puffin.co.uk
eviews.poems.jokes.authorevents.audioclips
www.puffin.co.uk.www.p   co.uk.www.puffin.co.uk
nterviews.e-mailupdates.bookinfo.competitions.news

www.puffin.co.uk

ames.sneakpreviews.adventure.bestsellers.fun
www.puffin.co.uk.www.puffin.co.uk.www.puffin.co.uk
ookinfo.competitions.news.games.sneakpreviews
www.puffin.co.uk.www.puffin.co.uk.www.puffin.co.uk
dventure.bestsellers.fun.coollinks.freestuff
www.puffin.co.uk.www.puffin.co.uk.www.puffin.co.uk
xplore.yourshout.awards.toptips.authorinfo
www.puffin.co.uk.www.puffin.co.uk.www.puffin.co.uk
reatbooks.greatbooks.greatbooks.greatbooks
www.puffin.co.uk.www.puffin.co.uk.www.puffin.co.uk
eviews.poems.jokes.authorevents.audioclips
www.puffin.co.uk.www.puffin.co.uk.www.puffin.co.uk

www.puffin.co.uk.www.puffin.co.uk.www.puffin.co.uk

bookinfo.competitions.news.games.sneakpreviews

www.puffin.co.uk.www.puffin.co.uk.www.puffin.co.uk

adventure.bestsellers.fun.coollinks.freestuf

www.puffin.co.uk.www.puffin.co.uk.www.puffin.co.uk

explore.yourshout.awards.toptips.authorinfo

www.puffin.co.uk.www.puffin.co.uk.www.puffin.co.uk

greatbooks.greatbooks.greatbooks.greatbooks

www.puffin.co.uk.www.puffin.co.uk.www.puffin.co.uk

reviews.poems.jokes.authorevents.audioclips

www.puffin.co.uk.www.puffin.co.uk.www.puffin.co.uk

interviews.e-mailupdates.bookinfo.competitions.news

www.puffin.co.uk

games.sneakpreviews.adventure.bestsellers.fun

www.puffin.co.uk.www.puffin.co.uk.www.puffin.co.uk

bookinfo.competitions.news.games.sneakpreviews

www.puffin.co.uk.www.puffin.co.uk.www.puffin.co.uk

adventure.bestsellers.fun.coollinks.freestuf

www.puffin.co.uk.www.puffin.co.uk.www.puffin.co.uk

explore.yourshout.awards.toptips.authorinfo

www.puffin.co.uk.www.puffin.co.uk.www.puffin.co.uk

greatbooks.greatbooks.greatbooks.greatbooks

www.puffin.co.uk.www.puffin.co.uk.www.puffin.co.uk

reviews.poems.jokes.authorevents.audioclips

www.puffin.co.uk.www.puffin.co.uk.www.puffin.co.uk

www.puffin.co.uk.www.puffin.co.uk.www.puffin.co.uk
bookinfo.competitions.news.games.sneakpreviews
www.puffin.co.uk.www.puffin.co.uk.www.puffin.co.uk
adventure.bestsellers.fun.coollinks.freestuff
www.puffin.co.uk.www.puffin.co.uk.www.puffin.co.uk
explore.yourshout.awards.toptips.authorinfo
www.puffin.co.uk.www.puffin.co.uk.www.puffin.co.uk
greatbooks.greatbooks.greatbooks.greatbooks
www.puffin.co.uk.www.puffin.co.uk.www.puffin.co.uk
eviews.poems.jokes.authorevents.audioclips
www.puffin.co.uk.www.puffin.co.uk.www.puffin.co.uk
nterviews.e-mailupdates.bookinfo.competitions.news

www.puffin.co.uk

games.sneakpreviews.adventure.bestsellers.fun
www.puffin.co.uk.www.puffin.co.uk.www.puffin.co.uk
bookinfo.competitions.news.games.sneakpreviews
www.puffin.co.uk.www.puffin.co.uk.www.puffin.co.uk
adventure.bestsellers.fun.coollinks.freestuff
www.puffin.co.uk.www.puffin.co.uk.www.puffin.co.uk
explore.yourshout.awards.toptips.authorinfo
www.puffin.co.uk.www.puffin.co.uk.www.puffin.co.uk
greatbooks.greatbooks.greatbooks.greatbooks
www.puffin.co.uk.www.puffin.co.uk.www.puffin.co.uk
eviews.poems.jokes.authorevents.audioclips
www.puffin.co.uk.www.puffin.co.uk.www.puffin.co.uk

www.puffin.co.uk.www.puffin.co.uk.www.puffin.co.uk

bookinfo.competitions.news.games.sneakpreviews

www.puffin.co.uk.www.puffin.co.uk.www.puffin.co.uk

adventure.bestsellers.fun.coollinks.freestuf

www.puffin.co.uk.www.puffin.co.uk.www.puffin.co.uk

explore.yourshout.awards.toptips.authorinfo

www.puffin.co.uk.www.puffin.co.uk.www.puffin.co.uk

greatbooks.greatbooks.greatbooks.greatbooks

www.puffin.co.uk.www.puffin.co.uk.www.puffin.co.uk

reviews.poems.jokes.authorevents.audioclips

www.puffin.co.uk.www.puffin.co.uk.www.puffin.co.uk

interviews.e-mailupdates.bookinfo.competitions.news

www.puffin.co.uk

games.sneakpreviews.adventure.bestsellers.fun

www.puffin.co.uk.www.puffin.co.uk.www.puffin.co.uk

bookinfo.competitions.news.games.sneakpreviews

www.puffin.co.uk.www.puffin.co.uk.www.puffin.co.uk

adventure.bestsellers.fun.coollinks.freestuf

www.puffin.co.uk.www.puffin.co.uk.www.puffin.co.uk

explore.yourshout.awards.toptips.authorinfo

www.puffin.co.uk.www.puffin.co.uk.www.puffin.co.uk

greatbooks.greatbooks.greatbooks.greatbooks

www.puffin.co.uk.www.puffin.co.uk.www.puffin.co.uk

reviews.poems.jokes.authorevents.audioclips

www.puffin.co.uk.www.puffin.co.uk.www.puffin.co.uk

www.puffin.co.uk.www.puffin.co.uk.www.puffin.co.uk

ookinfo.competitions.news.games.sneakpreviews

www.puffin.co.uk.www.puffin.co.uk.www.puffin.co.uk

dventure.bestsellers.fun.coollinks.freestuff

www.puffin.co.uk.www.puffin.co.uk.www.puffin.co.uk

xplore.yourshout.awards.toptips.authorinfo

www.puffin.co.uk.www.puffin.co.uk.www.puffin.co.uk

reatbooks.greatbooks.greatbooks.greatbooks

www.puffin.co.uk.www.puffin.co.uk.www.puffin.co.uk

eviews.poems.jokes.authorevents.audioclips

ww.puffin.co.uk.www.p   .co.uk.www.puffin.co.uk

nterviews.e-mailupdates.bookinfo.competitions.news

www.puffin.co.uk

ames.sneakpreviews.adventure.bestsellers.fun

ww.puffin.co.uk.www.puffin.co.uk.www.puffin.co.uk

ookinfo.competitions.news.games.sneakpreviews

www.puffin.co.uk.www.puffin.co.uk.www.puffin.co.uk

dventure.bestsellers.fun.coollinks.freestuff

www.puffin.co.uk.www.puffin.co.uk.www.puffin.co.uk

xplore.yourshout.awards.toptips.authorinfo

www.puffin.co.uk.www.puffin.co.uk.www.puffin.co.uk

reatbooks.greatbooks.greatbooks.greatbooks

www.puffin.co.uk.www.puffin.co.uk.www.puffin.co.uk

eviews.poems.jokes.authorevents.audioclips

www.puffin.co.uk.www.puffin.co.uk.www.puffin.co.uk

Read more in Puffin

For complete information about books available from Puffin – and Penguin – and how to
order them, contact us at the appropriate address below. Please note that for copyright
reasons the selection of books varies from country to country.

www.puffin.co.uk

In the United Kingdom: Please write to Dept EP, Penguin Books Ltd,
Bath Road, Harmondsworth, West Drayton, Middlesex UB7 ODA

In the United States: Please write to Penguin Putnam Inc., P.O. Box 12289,
Dept B, Newark, New Jersey 07101–5289 or call 1–800–788–6262

In Canada: Please write to Penguin Books Canada Ltd,
10 Alcorn Avenue, Suite 300, Toronto, Ontario M4V 3B2

In Australia: Please write to Penguin Books Australia Ltd,
P.O. Box 257, Ringwood, Victoria 3134

In New Zealand: Please write to Penguin Books (NZ) Ltd,
Private Bag 102902, North Shore Mail Centre, Auckland 10

In India: Please write to Penguin Books India Pvt Ltd,
11 Panscheel Shopping Centre, Panscheel Park, New Delhi 110 017

In the Netherlands: Please write to Penguin Books Netherlands bv,
Postbus 3507, NL–1001 AH Amsterdam

In Germany: Please write to Penguin Books Deutschland GmbH,
Metzlerstrasse 26, 60594 Frankfurt am Main

In Spain: Please write to Penguin Books S. A., Bravo Murillo 19,
1° B, 28015 Madrid

In Italy: Please write to Penguin Italia s.r.l.,
Via Felice Casati 20, I–20124 Milano

In France: Please write to Penguin France S. A.,
17 rue Lejeune, F–31000 Toulouse

In Japan: Please write to Penguin Books Japan, Ishikiribashi Building,
2–5–4, Suido, Bunkyo-ku, Tokyo 112

In South Africa: Please write to Longman Penguin Southern Africa (Pty) Ltd,
Private Bag X08, Bertsham 2013